HIS HEART
FOR THE TRUSTING

HIS HEART FOR THE TRUSTING

•

Lisa Mondello

AVALON BOOKS
NEW YORK

Library of Congress Catalog Card Number: 2001119826
ISBN 0-8034-9524-2

Published by Thomas Bouregy & Co., Inc.
160 Madison Avenue, New York, NY 10016

PRINTED IN THE UNITED STATES OF AMERICA
ON ACID-FREE PAPER
BY HADDON CRAFTSMEN, BLOOMSBURG, PENNSYLVANIA

For Maria, Tina, Linda, and Torry.
Much love and hugs!
Your sister, Lisa

Chapter One

What a homecoming, Sara. First day back in Texas in years and you crash the town social.

Sara Lightfoot chuckled at the nervous energy racing through her veins. She never thought coming home would be easy, but she certainly hadn't expected this much anxiety.

When she had first received Mandy's letter telling her she'd come back to Texas, Sara had gotten the bug to come home. *Safety in numbers*, Mandy had said. *No one will expect it.*

Yeah, right! She hadn't always done the unexpected, but this time she was sure her arrival would cause enough of a stir that heads would turn and a flurry of whispers would race across the lawn like a brush fire on a dry Texas day.

It wasn't *that* big a deal and she didn't relish the kind of attention that was sure to come her way. She was coming home to a place she never should have left. But when all was said and done, leaving had made her appreciate the home she had fled—the Apache reservation where she'd grown up.

As she drove down the endless highway toward Steerage Rock, Sara smiled to herself. She hadn't fled this time. This time she had chosen to leave L.A. and had shed a little piece of herself in the process. She'd given up her old life and taken back her family name. That was the first of many steps she hoped would bring her closer to home.

Her divorce from Dave was now final. Another huge step. Going home to reclaim a life she'd thrown away years before like a worn-out dress was the next step. She only hoped that old life would want her back as much as she wanted to be back.

Mandy had insisted it would and Sara clung to that hope.

Main Street looked exactly as it had the day she and Dave had walked into the Justice of the Peace's office downtown and had gotten married. As she drove past City Hall, she took the cold and lonely feeling that swept through her and pushed it aside. She hadn't thought it lonely the day of her marriage. After all, she had Dave. What more could she need? He was going to make all her childhood dreams come true. Funny how dreams turned out . . .

She heaved a heavy sigh as she reached the intersection for the main road leading to the Double T Ranch. Anticipation raced through her, setting her hands to trembling. Thank goodness Mandy had gone against her wishes and come to L.A. for a spontaneous visit. If she hadn't, Lord knows she would still be caught in the prison Dave had neatly built for her.

Sara took a left turn, her mind reeling with the anticipation of seeing family for the first time in almost nine years coupled with fear of their reaction.

As she sped past the red brick elementary school, she pulled over and parked the car on the grass near a chain link fence, feeling the *whoosh* of a speeding car on the opposite side of the road. Someone was in a hurry to get out of town, she thought. She'd had enough of that in L.A., where it seemed everyone was in a hurry. Out here, she'd have time. Time to heal her wounds and build back a life she'd thrown away.

A cluster of children played in the park and she had to smile. She'd always loved children. And they had always loved her stories. After volunteering at a daycare in L.A., sharing her Native American heritage with the children through stories, she decided it was time to reconnect with a piece of her that had been missing. Sure there were elementary schools and parks in L.A. and all over the world. She could have gone anywhere. But this . . . this was home.

A patch of open Texas sky stretched long and wide above the Double T Ranch. Mitch Broader adjusted his straw hat and took a moment to enjoy the view from where he was sitting, straddling a long beam of wood. Void of a single cloud, the deep cerulean space above him felt like a warm cozy blanket.

His face slipped into a grin that he couldn't hold back. It was a perfect day. They'd get all their work done with time to spare before any bad weather could say different. This kind of luck had been following Mitch Broader ever since he'd bought his share in the Double T's new rodeo school nearly a year ago. That one small step would bring him closer to fulfilling a dream he'd had ever since the first day he'd driven those long roads from the Amarillo airport with his grandfather.

Leaning forward on the sturdy beam, he waited for the crew of cowboys down on the ground to pass him and Beau Gentry, his longtime friend and now partner in the Double T's rodeo school, another beam to slip in place. This barn they were raising would give them plenty of room to house the horses they needed to run the school and bring him one step closer to the day when he'd have his own ranch, a dream he'd had since he'd come to Texas.

Of course, back then, when he was still a gangly green boy from Baltimore, Mitch hadn't understood the hard work and dedication it would take to own a spread. After years of working alongside some well-seasoned Texas cowboys, he knew. He'd listened and learned his lessons well. Having a piece of the Double T's new rodeo training school might not be the same as owning his own ranch, but it was a step in the right direction. And for now, that suited Mitch just fine. He wasn't in a hurry.

When this crew—mostly volunteers from surrounding ranches and neighbors who'd come out for the event like it was a square dance social—was done putting all the pieces of this post-and-beam barn together, when the last spike was hammered deep and secure into the fine wood, they would all celebrate. A party the size of Texas with all the food and fixin's he'd come to enjoy.

Dancing and women. Yeah, there would be plenty of that, too. And that was the fun part of being a cowboy.

"Yo, Mitch!"

He peered down from the beam he was holding onto, toward the sound of a familiar female voice. A drop of sweat from his brown forehead followed gravity and imbedded itself in his eye, causing it to sting. He had to blink twice before he could focus.

"I'm kind of hung up, Mandy. Want to wait a sec?" he called back to the blond-haired woman staring up at him through squinted eyes. Mandy held her arched back with both hands, clearly uncomfortable in the heat as she was nearly seven months pregnant with her first baby. There'd been a time, early on when he'd first arrived at the Double T Ranch, that he'd thought Mandy Morgan was the cutest little creature he'd ever laid eyes on. Still sporting one heck of an adolescent broken heart, he'd set himself up for more heartache when she up and fell in love with Beau, only to leave and never return to the ranch until last summer. Within the last year she'd become Mandy Morgan Gentry, Beau's bride.

Mitch reached for one end of the beam being eased his way by the ground crew and slipped it cleanly into the prenotched hole.

"Ah, Mitch?" Mandy called again. "If it was just me, I'd have no problem waiting on you. But I don't think this is something that can wait."

"You ain't in labor or anythin', darlin', are you?" Beau asked quickly, ready to jump down from the beam he was straddling to aid his wife, his face panic-stricken. "The doctor said you were supposed to take it easy to keep from having any more contractions."

"Cool your jets, Beau. I'm doing just fine," she said with a chuckle and a twinkle in her eye that made instant relief register on Beau's suntanned face. Pointing a finger at Mitch, she urged, "You're wanted in the house. Pronto."

Mitch couldn't help but stare as Mandy spun on her heels, with as much grace as a woman in her condition could, and waddled back to the main farmhouse.

Beau chuckled from the other end of the beam. "What'd you do, Mitch? Forget to scrape the muck off your boots before walking into the house again?"

"It wouldn't be the first time. Corrine made it more than clear she'd have my head on a spit if I ruined that new carpet in the dining room."

"Never known Corrine to tell a lie."

Mitch couldn't help but laugh. Corrine Promise was a small woman, but the last two years had tested her strength—had tested them all—and she'd come out of it victoriously. The matriarch of the ranch, even though she'd rather be holed up in her art studio with her hands in clay or paints than within ten feet of a cow, she was the epitome of an old-time pioneer woman in spirit. While her husband, as owner of the Double T Ranch, might be in charge of running the daily business, there was no doubt it was Corrine who was in charge of the Promise home.

Mitch adjusted his straw cowboy hat on his head, feeling another trickle of sweat make a journey down the side of his face before dropping off and hitting his already sweat-soaked white T-shirt. He finished nailing the steel spike into the beam to keep it in its place.

He glanced at his handiwork with appreciation. If done right, this barn would be standing long after he was nothing more than dust on this earth.

"Wish me luck," he muttered in somewhat of a groan as he climbed down from the skeleton of the barn.

Beau's laughter faded as Mitch hiked through the crowd of neighbors and friends gathered to help with the festivities. A bundle of women stood gabbing under a shady tree about something intense as they poured pink lemonade to pass out to the chain of people working on the barn. They paid no attention to him as he grabbed one of the filled paper cups lining the table and drank it down before shooting it into a garbage can.

Mitch drew in a pensive breath before he reached the screen door. Pausing, he scraped his boots extra hard on the doormat with a little more care than usual before walking into the house.

"Would it help if I said sorry for whatever I did, Corrine?"

He heard her lighthearted chuckle and let out a breath of relief. How much trouble could he really be in if she still held her humor?

"Do what you like," Corrine called back to him from inside, "but I'm afraid it'll do no good."

He made a face and groaned audibly. *What on earth had he done this time?*

"You've got to be kidding," Mitch said just moments later, still not believing the bombshell that had just exploded in his face. He swayed for a second, and then slumped against the wall. *It was a joke. It had to be!*

Corrine held the tiny infant in her arms and eyed him. Not a trace of humor on her face. "Do I look like I'm kidding?"

"You've got to be . . ."

"Hard to believe, isn't it? Mitch Broader a daddy. Hearts will be breaking wide open now that Mitchell Broader is no longer footloose and fancy free," Mandy chimed in. "You're gonna be changing diapers instead of picking up women after bringing the cows home."

"This is a sick joke."

Corrine shrugged as she blew a fallen tendril of hair from her forehead. "Maybe, but we're not the one playing it on you."

"We're not into cruel and unusual punishment. Even for you," said Mandy.

"Thanks a lot, Mandy," he said, his mouth skewing into a wry grin.

She chuckled softly as she peered over the baby Corrine held in her arms and crooned softly. "Any time."

"She actually said . . . Lillian said that I'm this kid's daddy? I mean . . . and then she just . . . left? She left the kid here for me to raise?" His throat constricted and he was finding it hard to breathe. He was glad there was a solid wall behind him to keep him standing.

"Did you see the dust cloud running down the driveway? The woman was in quite a hurry to escape."

"I'll just bet." His laugh held no humor. That would be typical Lillian. If it involved money, Lillian was in a hurry. "Did anyone else talk with her? Did she say when she was coming back?"

"Nope and with all the commotion today, no one would have noticed her, anyway. I came into the house to check on the lemon pies and she was just there sitting at the kitchen table like the rest of the chairs. I have no idea how long she'd been sitting there. All she said was this was your baby and your responsibility now. She didn't say anything about coming back for him."

Corrine stood up from the worn couch she'd been sitting on, rocking the sleeping baby in her arms. She padded softly over to Mitch and held the child out to him. Her arms hung in the air. What did she expect him to do?

"He's truly an adorable child. Don't you want to hold your son?" she asked with the kind of warmth and compassion he'd come to love about her. Except this time, he didn't want to see it.

His son? Had she really called this warm little bundle his son? He looked at the baby boy dressed in a Baltimore Orioles baseball outfit and little sock booties, then back at Corrine and at the baby again.

Corrine chuckled softly so as not to rouse the baby. "He's not going to do anything. I promise you that. It's a lot easier to hold him for the first time while he's asleep. Pretty soon he'll probably be crying for something."

"I don't know anything about holding a baby."

He was vaguely aware of Mandy coming into the living room, holding a freshly laundered white T-shirt. He'd somehow missed the fact that she'd left the room for a moment.

"You are *not* touching this precious baby wearing that sweaty shirt," Mandy insisted. "Put this one on."

He did as he was told, handing the shirt he'd been wearing to Mandy, who took it between her fingertips and walked back to the laundry room.

He shook his head. "I can't do this. There's got to be a mistake."

"He's a baby, Mitch, not a bomb. Although he'll probably deposit something explosive in his diaper real soon," Mandy said sympathetically.

Corrine placed the baby in the crook of his arm and closed his hand around him to keep the baby snug. "Don't worry. You've encountered worse messes in the barn. You can handle a little diaper."

"Now this I've got to see," Mandy said crossing her arms across her chest and resting them on her ample belly.

He didn't know what irked him more. The fact that Lillian had pulled another fast one on him by dropping off some kid at the ranch and claiming it was his son or the fact that Mandy and Corrine seemed to be taking such pleasure in something that was obviously meant to make him squirm.

"I know it's a shock," Mandy started to say, but Mitch cut her off.

"That's quite the understatement."

"But you do know who this Lillian person is, right?" Mandy asked. "I mean, she's not some stranger who happened to drive on by?"

No, Lillian was definitely not a stranger. "I know her."

"Then is it possible she's telling the truth? This is your son?" Corrine asked.

He stared down at the baby and mentally counted the months since he'd last been in Baltimore. The last time he'd seen Lillian.

"It's a possibility."

Corrine shrugged and smiled. "Well, then there you have it. Looks like we have a baby on the ranch sooner than we thought."

Mitch stared down at the baby. No, it couldn't be. A baby?

Corrine's sympathetic voice carved its way into his shock. "I really hate to do this to you, but I've got food in the oven that needs my attention." Corrine left the room.

"I wish I could help you right now, too," Mandy said. "But we're already stretched with all this cooking, especially now that Alice has gone home with a migraine."

Mitch couldn't find air. "Wait . . . wait . . . you can't leave me alone with . . . with—"

Corrine pointed to the yard. "Do you see that crowd out there? They're here for us. They didn't have to leave their ranches to do this, but they're here. I've got a lot of mouths to feed and come sundown after the work they've done they are going to be mighty hungry for some food. I wish it were different but we can't help you baby-sit right now."

Mandy moved past him, eyeing the baby with dreamy eyes. "A little later, when things slow down some, I can give you a break."

Mitch started gently bouncing the baby as he stirred, looking so tiny in his big arms. "What do I . . . what's his name?"

Corrine poked her head in for just a second and said, "Jonathan."

Then they were gone. And he was alone. With a baby.

Sara brought her sedan to a full stop at the gate announcing the Double T Ranch. It had been a long time since she'd visited Hank and Corrine Promise. Their spread was bigger than she'd remembered. But then a lot of changing happens in nine years. Mandy had mentioned hard times last year when she'd visited, something to do with Hank's health, but by the look of things it seemed the hard times had past. She was glad for that.

She hit the gas pedal and pushed past the gate. A long string of cars and pickups trucks lined the side of the drive. As she approached, she saw a large green and white striped tent set up in the back yard with tables and chairs arranged beneath it. It wasn't until she got closer that she saw a team of people engrossed in erecting a post-and-beam barn.

It was a real, honest to goodness old-fashioned barn raising. *Now that was something you didn't see every day in Los Angeles.*

There were people crawling all over the yard like ants picking up crumbs at a picnic. Sara parked her rental at the end of the line and walked along the row of cars leading to the festivities, passing grazing cows. The smell of manure and freshly mown hay drying in the sun filled her nose.

She should have changed into shorts and sneakers before she'd left the airport, she thought, feeling sweat trickle down the center of her chest. Her coral silk sleeveless blouse and pants were clinging to her skin after the long ride from the airport.

Clutched by anxiety and the overwhelming desire to run, she made a beeline for the house before anyone recognized her. With any luck, she'd spot Mandy first and have a private meeting before barging in on her parents. Odds were her mother was here already, having been the housekeeper at the Double T for more than fifteen years.

The screen door slammed, drawing her attention to the house. There'd be fewer people inside on such a hot day. Maybe she'd be able to find Mandy there before anyone spotted her.

Slipping past a group of blue-haired ladies diving into a pitcher of iced tea under a low hanging cottonwood tree, Sara rushed up the brick path to the front door that faced the driveway. As she approached, she heard the plaintive sound of a baby crying and the deep groan of a male voice. An extremely exasperated male voice.

The urgency of that voice had her bolting into the house without knocking.

The tall, dark-haired man pacing the living room and bouncing the baby was much too pre-occupied with trying to stop the baby's crying to notice her. He had his broad back to her, but it couldn't possibly be Beau, Sara quickly decided. She'd seen pictures of the wedding when Mandy had visited. Even with his back turned, she knew he looked different. And Mandy's baby wasn't due for at least another two months, according to her last letter.

Dropping her purse on the oak end table, Sara advanced across the carpeted floor, thinking more about the poor infant than startling the man with her silent entry.

"Keep that up and you'll be smelling baby vomit on your boots for the next month," she said.

The man swung around with the sound of her voice. It wasn't Beau, but she did know his face. She'd seen him before, but she couldn't quite place where. "Oh, thank God someone is here," he said, relief bursting to life in his sun-tanned face.

His bright eyes were a deep sapphire blue with flecks of gold and gray that reminded Sara of sunset and sunrise all in one. Although his face was a bronze color from the long days spent in the Texas sun, his nose was slightly red and peeling, a testament to his fair skin. Sweat lined his dark brows as they creased.

"They all left me alone. He's been crying and I have no idea what to do."

"Poor baby," she said, standing near enough now to stroke her finger across the baby's smooth cheek.

"Thanks."

"No, I meant the baby. His mother should be brought up on charges for leaving this child with the likes of you."

The man heaved a sigh. "At the moment, I couldn't agree with you more. Do you know anything about babies?"

"I know it's not good to bounce him around so much. It'll give him an upset stomach."

"He's been crying forever."

Sara rolled her eyes and couldn't help but smile. Cowboys had the stomach for castrating a bull but some were so helpless when it came to babies. She actually felt sorry for him. "I'm sure it only seems that way."

"No, I swear. And I don't know what he wants."

"If he's been crying a long time, he may have colic."

"Colic. You mean like a horse?" he croaked.

Sara chuckled quietly at the horrified look her gave her, thinking how good it felt to do that after so long. "Yeah, something like that."

The man gulped. "Sometimes we have to put down horses with colic."

"Trust me, you're not going to have to do that to the baby. When was the last time he had a bottle?"

He looked at her blankly. "A bottle?"

"Yeah, has he been fed? You know, formula you put in a bottle to feed the baby? You're not going to give him a slab of steak fresh off the grill at his age. Or maybe his mother is nursing?"

The man's broad shoulders sagged. "Look, I know how to raise cows. I'm an imbecile when it comes to a baby."

Sara quirked an eyebrow. "So it seems."

She reached out and rescued the baby from the man and stretched his belly down over the length of her arm, cooing to soothe his cries. With a practiced hand, she checked his diaper to find that it was still dry.

"I take it this is not your baby."

His blue eyes grazed the baby and for a moment he looked a little lost. With a sigh, he said, "Can you help me?"

Sara glanced around the living room in search of a diaper bag. "See if there is a bottle in that diaper bag. If there is, bring it into the kitchen."

Holding the baby with one arm, she took a stainless steel pan from the iron rack above the stove and filled it with hot tap water. The kitchen was filled with delicious smells of food that suddenly made her remember she hadn't eaten anything since that morning.

The man came into the kitchen, rifling through the diaper bag until he pulled out a bottle filled with baby formula. Taking it from his hands, she placed it in the pan to warm, glad that her time volunteering at the daycare center back in L.A. made her feel useful here. It also took her mind off her anxiety for the time being.

"Aren't you going to give the bottle to the baby?"

"How would you like to eat a cold steak for dinner?" she said softly, not wanting to jar the baby. Although he was still crying, the sobs weren't as extreme. After a few minutes she pulled the bottle from the water, testing it on her arm as she walked back into the living room. She perched herself on the edge of the sofa and placed the nipple at the baby's mouth. Immediately the infant took hold and started suckling.

"Oh, thank God," the man said, running both hands over his head as silence filled the air. "I thought he was never going to stop."

"He was just hungry. That's all. Babies can't skip meals like grownups can."

"You must have had a lot of practice doing this. You're a natural."

"I know a thing or two about children."

"What did you do, raise all your brothers and sisters?"

"I volunteered at a daycare for awhile."

The man sat on the opposite end of the sofa and appeared to finally relax a little. "Daycare, huh? I'll have to remember that. I'm eternally in your debt."

Sara tossed him a wry grin. "That's a bit extreme, don't you think? All I did was give him a bottle."

"You wouldn't say that if you'd been here the last half hour."

He was staring at her for the first time, now that he wasn't occupied with a crying baby. She shifted uncomfortably as his blue eyes pierced her and then seemed to brighten just a notch.

"I know you. We've met before." His smile was of the high-wattage variety, complete with perfect white teeth and dimple marking his cheek.

Sara had thought she'd recognized him and now that he seemed familiar with her, she realized she must have seen him some point.

"I'd offer to shake your hand, but they're a little busy. I'm Sara Green—I mean Sara Lightfoot," she said, catching herself when she almost gave him her former married name.

His face lit up. "We have met. A long time ago here at the ranch. Alice's daughter, right?"

She nodded. "How do you know—"

"Mitch Broader. I started working here at the ranch on weekends my last year of high school."

"Mitch." She thought back to the years before she'd run away, before she met Dave and her world shifted so rapidly. "I remember a tall lanky kid who had a colossal crush on Mandy who always poked around the barn whenever we were around."

He shot her a lopsided grin that made her insides

flutter just a bit. "And here I thought I was being charming."

Sara chuckled, amazed that it felt this good.

"Your mother didn't mention anything about you coming home."

Anxiety hit her square in the stomach. "She didn't know." Trying to deflect his attention from her, she asked, "What's the baby's name?"

"Jonathan."

"Well, hello there, Jonathan," she crooned as she stared down at the baby in her arms.

"Is his mom outside helping with the barn raising?"

Mitch groaned. "If I know Lillian, she's probably out raising Cain."

She felt a frown crease her forehead. "Then, this is your baby?"

"I . . . I'm not sure."

"You don't know?"

Mitch's face grew tight. "He's my responsibility right now. Beyond that I know about as much as you do."

It was none of her business anyway. "I'm sorry. I didn't mean to pry."

"Forget it. At least you got him to stop crying. I never knew how good silence sounded."

She looked down at the tiny infant, who seemed drugged by the formula he'd just consumed. "He looks just like you, you know."

"He's a baby. All babies look alike," Mitch said, the tension back in his face.

But it instantly vanished as the screen door slammed

shut and the two of them looked up at the doorway leading to the kitchen.

Sara's stomach wound into a tight knot and she quickly handed the sleeping baby back to Mitch.

"Sara? Sara, is that you?"

Chapter Two

She knew the voice without even looking at her face. It sent a rush of childhood memories flowing through her, settling in her heart.

When she turned back to the doorway, Sara found Mandy standing there.

"Uncle Hank thought he saw you walk into the house, but Aunt Corrine said it couldn't possibly be. But I knew better," she said quietly, her hands clutched together over her ample belly.

Sara shrugged. "You didn't tell anyone about your visit to L.A.?"

"You asked me not to," Mandy said, coming into the room now. Sara stood in front of Mandy as her friend looked her up and down.

"Gosh, you look terrific. You cut your hair shorter."

Sara's fingers instinctively went to her much shorter hair. Dave had said that her long hair was what attracted her to him during the short time they dated, but it was the first thing he'd insisted she change when they moved to Los Angeles. He didn't want her to be the little Indian girl he'd fallen in love with. She wasn't glamorous that way. Or so he'd said. At the time, she agreed so she'd cut her hair and colored it. Back then she just wanted to please him. Now she hated herself more than him for it.

"I'm still deciding on it."

"No, it looks perfect for you. Come here and give me a hug."

"It's so good to see you again, Mandy." The initial anxiety of coming home and facing her past was beginning to ebb. Sara had known it would be difficult to see familiar faces again, but seeing Mandy made things easier.

"You didn't tell my mother?"

Mandy pulled from her embrace, still holding her shoulders. "No one knew. You weren't certain you'd be coming so I didn't see any reason to get anyone's hopes up."

Sara gave a wry laugh. "I suppose with my track record that was a good idea."

"Never mind about that. It took a lot of guts to leave L.A."

"No. Leaving L.A. was easy. Leaving Dave . . . now that was harder than I imagined."

Sara and Mandy seemed to fall into such companionable conversation that the years apart didn't seem so long, and yet, it felt like forever.

Mandy reached out and hugged her again. Emotion

rose in Sara's throat and lodged there, leaving her to think about how very different her life would be now if Mandy hadn't valued their friendship enough to seek her out again in L.A.

"I'm sweating," Mandy said, her voice cracking, letting Sara know that emotion had gotten the best of her as well.

"I don't care," she replied, laughing through her tears.

"I'm going to ruin your silk suit."

"I'll buy another one. I've missed you."

It was one thing to be greeted so warmly by Mandy. It would be something altogether different with her parents. The way she'd left and how she'd lived since leaving the reservation had left a lot to be desired. Family was so important to the Apache people, and she'd tossed hers away like a piece of crumpled newspaper.

"My mother, is she here?"

Mandy glanced at her, tears clinging to her eyelashes, and shook her head. "She was here earlier, but wasn't feeling all that well. Corrine sent her home. She'd been working so hard to get ready for the barn raising and . . . well . . ."

"What?" Fear settled deep in the pit of Sara's stomach. "Is something wrong with her health?"

"Oh, no. Nothing like that. She's just been tired lately. And you know Alice. She's such a workhorse. You can't get her to slow down enough to take a breath."

Vaguely disappointed that she'd missed her mother, Sara contemplated her next step. She was going to have to surprise her parents by going to the reservation. It would have been easier, she realized, to meet her mother at the Double T with the support of close friends. Now she'd have to face her family alone.

Mitch felt out of place watching Sara and Mandy's homecoming. So, instead of eavesdropping, he focused his attention on a homecoming of a different kind: the sleeping baby in his arms.

What he did know about the bond between children and parents? His own childhood hadn't been the greatest. If this was his kid, as Lillian claimed, wouldn't he be able to feel it? Wouldn't there be some spark of emotion inside of him for this child?

His pulse pounded against his skull like a jackhammer just thinking about it. If this was his kid, he fully intended to do his part. But what if it was just another one of Lillian's ploys? He'd learned firsthand that she didn't care much about whom she hurt when she wanted something. The only question was, what did she want?

Mitch didn't think even Lillian would stoop to adding an innocent child to one of her schemes.

Mitch couldn't help but feel sorry for the baby. If this wasn't his son, then this baby would be mighty lonely without a dad. And that was something Mitch knew about first hand.

But if it *was* his kid? He didn't have a clue of what to do. There was so much work at the ranch now that they'd expanded to include the new rodeo school. Hank, Mandy's uncle and owner of the Double T Ranch, was hardly in a position to take on more even though last year's bypass surgery had brought him back up to speed again. No one, especially Mitch, was willing to risk him having a relapse.

Mitch didn't have much of a choice. He'd have to hire a ranch hand on his own and pay him out of his own wages from the ranch to take on some of his work. It wasn't right to expect Hank to take on that responsibility.

Or a nanny. Yeah, that would work, Mitch decided as he carefully held the baby so as not to rouse him. The last thing he needed was a screaming repeat of the half hour before Sara had arrived. Much as he hated to admit it, he couldn't do this alone. He'd have to get someone to take care of the kid so he could do his job.

His eyes were drawn to the baby in his arms. He was warm and smelled of something sour and something sweet like baby powder. Jonathan was his name. He looked so miniature in his arms, as if he were a toy baby doll, not a real baby.

Mitch wished he knew more about babies so he could figure out if this baby was really his. He didn't see any resemblance to him. Sara had. But looks alone didn't make him the father.

This wasn't exactly how he'd envisioned working the ranch. Somehow having a kid strapped to him wasn't part of his plans.

"First thing we need to do is find your momma, little one," he said quietly. "Don't you worry. We'll get to the bottom of this."

With the sound of his voice, the baby's eyes flew open and he started to squirm. His little face skewed and turned bright crimson with one look at Mitch and in an instant Jonathan let out a howl to beat the wolves.

"Perfect." Mitch yanked himself off the sofa and raced to the kitchen where he'd last heard Mandy and Sara, hoping he'd find Sara still there.

Sara turned around and immediately looked at the crying baby and then at Mitch. Tears glistened in her dark brown eyes and her shiny brown hair was slightly mussed from her embrace with Mandy. He felt like a jerk for asking for her help again.

"Now what did you do to him?" Sara said, sniffing.

"Nothing. He just woke up and looked at me."

"What did you expect, you're a stranger," she said in the same calm tone she'd used before when she'd first come into the house.

"You're a stranger too and he doesn't cry like that with you."

"Here, let me take him."

He handed Jonathan to Sara, feeling like a complete imbecile. In a skilled move, she transferred the baby to her shoulder and within a few seconds and some light tapping on his back with her fingers, his crying subsided. How on earth did she do that?

Frustrated, he threw up his hands in despair. "This is ridiculous. How can I possibly take care of a kid when I don't know a thing about them? I need to find Lillian."

"I wish I could be more help, Mitch," Mandy said, dreamily looking at the baby. "But I told you she just took off without saying a word about coming back."

He sighed, feeling dread and helplessness settle deep in the pit of his gut.

"His mother just left him?" Sara asked, horrified.

Mandy nodded. "That's right. Aunt Corrine tried to ask her but she headed for the door and said, 'I did my part by bringing him into the world, now it's Mitch's turn to take over.' She was gone before we could even figure out what had happened. She didn't waste time for even a last good-bye kiss for Jonathan."

He watched Sara holding the baby as if having a baby in her arms were as natural as breathing.

A sudden sadness was in her eyes when she spoke. "You know, Mitch, single parents do this all the time. I've seen it at the daycare. Mind you, it's not easy, but you can do it. You just have to figure out your options."

Yeah, he could do it. Hadn't he made it on his own so far? Growing up in an abusive home left him fiercely independent. He'd learned to rely on himself and it had gotten him this far. Now all he had to do was figure out how to manage it with a baby.

"Maybe so, but I'm going to need some help. Anyone with an ounce of sense can see that," Mitch said. "At least until I find Jonathan's mother."

"I can't speak for Corrine, but I'll help you any way that I can."

He smiled at Mandy's offer. "Thanks, Mandy, but I couldn't do that to you. In a few months you're going to have your hands full caring for your own baby."

Her hand went to her belly and she began to rub it.

"And I can't ask Corrine to watch him day in and day out. She has her own life, too."

"You don't have—" Mandy started to say before Mitch cut her off.

Holding up a hand, he said, "I know both of you will help me out when you can. I suspect Corrine will probably enjoy doting on a kid or two, by the way she's been going on about you being pregnant and all. I just can't ask you to take on the responsibility every day. That's my job."

"You could hire a nanny for when you work during the day," Sara said.

"And what about at night? A cowboy doesn't work a normal nine-to-five job."

Sara shrugged. "Then hire a live-in nanny. That way you can see the baby when you can and work when you have to. People do it and it works. You just have to find the right person you trust."

Mitch's lips tilted to a grin for the first time since he'd walked into the house and met his son. "The baby seems pretty content with you."

Sara shot an alarming gaze at him that reminded him of a deer blinded by headlights. Her eyes were now dry and for the first time, he really noticed them. They were a rich brown color that lit up when she looked at Jonathan. That baby looked as natural in her arms as the mountain range stretching out in the horizon.

But right now, her eyes flashed with a burst of lightning that made him suck in a breath.

"Oh, no. No, no," she said, shaking her head.

He forged on. "Why not?"

"Because I can't. That's all. I can't do it."

"Anyone can see taking care of a baby is way beyond my ability."

"No kidding. But I'm sorry I can't be the one to help you. After I leave here I'm going back to the reservation."

"For good?" Mandy asked.

Sara blew out a quick breath that hinted of dread. "We'll see how the reunion goes first. I'm not sure how they're going to feel having me back after all this time. Or if they'll truly believe I'm here to stay."

"You know, Sara, it would go a long way with your parents if you had a job."

"I want to be on the reservation. Being a storyteller and teaching the young people on the rez about our culture was the whole reason for leaving L.A."

"Are you sure?"

Sara didn't answer.

"Be careful what you wish for," Mandy went on. "Life in L.A. is quite different from Steerage Rock. Believe me, I know. It takes time to get used to the new pace. You were so eager to leave home before and you don't know how things are going to be when you get back. If you have a job, even if it is off the reservation, it'll prove to your family that you're home for good without committing you to the reservation until you know for sure how you'll feel being home."

"But if I don't go home—I mean all the way home—they'll never truly believe I've come home for good," said Sara. "No, I need to be on the reservation. For myself as well as for them.

"This baby is a dear," Sara continued, turning to Mitch and nuzzling the baby with her cheek. "But taking care of him is a full time responsibility and would demand all my time. To do it properly, and fit in with a rancher's hours, I'd need to live here."

"I've got the room. I'm in the middle of remodeling the house, but it's fit to live in."

Sara shook her head. "That's not the point. It would

take all of my time. When would I have time for the stories?"

"We could work around that. I'd make sure it worked."

But Mitch could tell he was losing this battle. It had been too easy a proposition. If Sara had agreed, it would have been the answer to his prayers, Mitch knew. But he wasn't going to let it get him down.

"There's nothing written in stone that says you can't stay here on the ranch and work things out with your parents before going back to the reservation for good," Mandy said.

Not ready to admit defeat, Mitch gave it one more try. "Look, Sara, I know you've got to do what you've got to do. I can respect that. This baby is just as unexpected for me as my asking you to watch him. But I can't work the ranch and be up all night with a baby. It just can't be done. I'd be eternally grateful if you'd consider doing it, if only until I can find someone permanent to replace you."

She quirked a thinly lined eyebrow and smiled, and his breath hitched in his throat. In theory, it could work. But having a beautiful woman like Sara Lightfoot in his house was going to be a major distraction.

"I thought you were already eternally grateful?"

Mitch's eyes gleamed as he gave Sara a slow smile. "I'll mean it this time, if you take the job."

Sara thought about it. Why did the idea of living under the same roof with Mitch Broader stir her so? Surely, it was just nerves. Nerves over seeing her family after so long and facing up to her past, she decided after a while.

She thought of the plans she made that had kept her

going during her divorce, the dreams of being a Native American storyteller, teaching the Apache culture to the young people on the reservation. None of that was set up yet. Why couldn't she take care of Jonathan for a little while as she arranged all the details?

"Okay," she finally said. When Mitch heaved a sigh of relief, Sara amended, "But this is only temporary. Just until I can set things up on the reservation. It'll give you time to get yourself used to handling the baby and to find someone permanent."

"It's a deal." He took her hand in his and she was surprised by its strength. His hand was rough, the color of the weather-beaten earth, and strong. The strength of his hand holding hers made her head spin. She wondered if she hadn't suddenly made a wager with the devil.

Sure, Mitch was a cowboy and cowboys worked sunup to sundown nonstop. None of the work was pretty. That accounted for the calluses on his palms and the dirt under his nails. But this wasn't work strength. It was something more.

She snatched her hand from his grip, uneasy with the slight tremble that quickened her heartbeat.

Mitch blew out a sigh of relief. "When can I get you moved in?"

Still feeling the effects of his touch, Sara teased, "Are you afraid I'll change my mind?"

"If you did, I'd do my best to change it back. I need you, Sara."

A quick burst of warm emotion spread through her chest like hot frosting on a toasted bun. Mitch needed her help with the baby. There was a time when she thought no one needed her. Her ex-husband had made it clear that he wanted her. Possessing her was more like it. But he'd never really needed her. The children she cared for at the daycare had needed her care, but it wasn't the same need they had for their parents.

Deep down, Sara had always thought that someday she'd have a loving home again. One that needed her and loved her. Mitch didn't love her, he was merely asking for her help in a sticky situation that was thrust upon him. He needed her to help him watch this little baby who was an innocent in a story she knew nothing about.

What makes a mother toss away a child? What did this child's mother go through that led her to leave her child on the doorstep of a father who didn't know him?

It wasn't her problem to figure it out. She wasn't staying very long anyway. Mitch didn't need her, but she could be of help. Feeling part of her old world again, even if she weren't on the reservation, would bring her closer to home.

"Like I said, I will watch the baby until you get settled. But tonight, I do have to go to the reservation and see my family. Can you manage until then?"

"Most of the cooking is under control now. I can watch Jonathan while you're gone, unless of course you want me to go with you," Mandy said.

Sara smiled even though her heart beat louder with each passing second. "Having you there as an ally would make things so much easier. But I have to do this one myself."

As Sara expected, her homecoming was both shocking and emotional. Apache people valued family ties.

Deep down she'd known her family wouldn't turn her away. The wind had carried her home, her father had said. The apprehension in her mother's eyes was apparent when she told them she was going back to the Double T. As she feared, they wouldn't believe she was truly home unless she remained on the reservation.

She wanted that, too.

There was time for all that, she decided on the drive back to Steerage Rock. Time for more healing and to put in place her plans to teach the young Apache children the stories of their culture, something she knew had been slipping away as the modern world clashed with old-time beliefs.

It was past eleven o'clock when she pulled up the main road to the Double T. Those who'd been participating in the barn raising had long since returned to their own homes. There were just empty tables and chairs on the back lawn to indicate their presence now. The main house was dark and Sara's eyes were immediately drawn to the lights in the bunkhouse out back.

She pulled her car up next to the pickup truck parked out front of the foreman's house and killed the ignition. As she stepped out of the car into the cool night air, she groaned. Jonathan was crying.

If tonight was any indication of how his life was going to be from now on, he was in deep trouble. Mitch stood helplessly on the other side of the room, leaning against the wood-grained wall he'd sanded and stained no less than two weeks ago, watching as Sara worked her magic to calm Jonathan once again.

Mandy had taken charge of Jonathan's care most of the time Sara had been at the reservation. Corrine had given her a break to eat and then passed the baby around for some of the woman to dote on.

Mitch marveled as Beau carried Jonathan around, announcing that he'd have a kid of his own in just a few short months. There was such joy in Beau's eyes that Mitch found himself a little jealous of his friend. He didn't feel that joy yet.

He wondered if he'd ever feel it when not ten minutes upon returning to his house after the festivities, Jonathan started fussing. When Sara had arrived, Mitch had been at the end of his rope. How could he possibly keep this baby?

"This is ridiculous. I need to go to Baltimore," he said finally.

Sara peered up at him from her seat in the rocking chair, her dark eyes filled with questions. But she said nothing.

"I need to find Jonathan's mother. His mother lives in Baltimore."

Sara nodded. "And his father lives right here."

Mitch shook his head and grunted his frustration. "I don't know that for sure."

"That's pretty apparent or you wouldn't feel compelled to take this child all the way back across the country after already coming such a long way."

Contemplating her words, he replied, "You don't think I should?"

"It's not my decision to make. I'm not Jonathan's parent."

He threw up his hands in frustration and dropped down on the sofa opposite her. "That's my point exactly. I don't know if I am either. I mean, yes, there is a possibility. But Lillian was no angel. We're no longer together because of it."

Sara was quiet for a moment, turning her sole attention to the baby who was finally falling asleep in her arms. When she lifted her head to gaze at Mitch, a lock of her black hair fell to her cheek, framing her face. His chest squeezed just seeing how beautiful she was.

None of this made any sense. Yesterday he was alone. He had his goals and he didn't need anyone. Now a baby and beautiful woman had moved into his house and suddenly nothing made any sense.

"There are some things you just know. It has nothing to do with DNA or names on a birth certificate. You just know. Do you believe this baby is really yours?"

Sara held the baby as if he was an extension of her, not him. What she was asking, he truly didn't have the answer to. He wished he did. It would make things so much easier now. When he looked at Jonathan, he saw a stranger, not someone who had come from him.

She seemed to sense his feelings. Her lips stretched into a slow grin that had him forgetting her words and concentrating only on her perfect mouth that at the moment looked far too kissable. "The uncles always say the answers can be found in the wind if you'll only listen. But deep down in your heart, I think you have your answer. You just have to ask yourself."

He couldn't help but smile. He knew nothing about tribal beliefs, even though Sara's family had been visiting the Double T for all the ten years he'd worked here. Something about what she was saying rang true.

"Here, take him," she said, lifting out of the rocking chair slowly and delicately padding across the room to where he was now sitting on the sofa. He took Jonathan in his arms, felt his heart beat strong and his arms tremble.

She settled down so close that the scent of her drifted to him, making him dizzy. What he was thinking had nothing to do with the baby in his arms and everything to do with the woman whose smooth and velvety voice took him by command.

"If you think you'll find the answers you want by going to Baltimore, then that is what you should do. But if you look at Jonathan and know in your heart that he is your son, what more proof do you need?"

Jonathan was impossibly lost in his arms. Mitch had helped birth many a farm animal, but he'd never held something so small and wondrously perplexing in his life. How could this tiny creature have come from him? It just didn't make any sense.

A lump lodged in his throat and seemed impossibly hard to swallow. "He does kinda look like me, doesn't he?"

Sara offered him a lopsided smile. "Dead ringer."

She laughed softly and Mitch's head started spinning. There was something acutely appealing about a woman who could read a man's mind the way Sara was reading his right now. It made him want to scoop her up into his arms and hold her, make the connection between them physical, real. This heady emotional zing was too much.

There was this . . . air between them, sizzling with an electric current that could burn the room down to ash. And she was looking up at him with light dancing in her rich brown eyes and all Mitch could think about was kissing her.

Jonathan stirred in his arms, kicking and adjusting himself in his sleep, and the connection was severed.

"You're going to need to get a bed for him," Sara said as she lightly stroked the almost-not-there hair on the baby's head.

Mitch swallowed hard. "Mandy had a cradle ready at the house for her baby. Beau started building it the moment he learned she was pregnant. He brought it in to use tonight."

"Jonathan won't be in a cradle for too long. Babies grow quickly. Besides, Mandy is going to be needing it soon anyway."

"I'll build him a crib."

He didn't know why, but this moment felt strangely familiar, like he'd been away on a journey and had just returned home after a long time. But that was ridiculous. Any familiarity he had with Sara had to be conjured up from memories of when he'd come to the Double T, before she'd run away.

He watched from the other side of the dark room as Sara put Jonathan in his cradle and rocked him. She softly sang a tune that was foreign to him, in a tongue he'd only heard when he was among the Apache people.

He'd attended attended countless rodeos with his grandfather, but only one on the reservation a few years back when Beau was still riding bronc. Other than that and the bits he'd learned from knowing Alice these last ten years, he knew nothing of Apache culture.

There was something earthy and pure about Sara, singing in her native tongue, caring for his son.

His son.

That was going to take some getting used to.

Chapter Three

It had been almost two weeks since Jonathan had arrived in his life and Sara had moved into his home. Mitch tried to hold onto the belief that Jonathan was in fact his son, but somehow, he just couldn't feel it. After a day of vaccines and veterinarian visits for the new horses he'd bought at auction, he was tired and looking forward to nothing more than going back to the quiet house he'd started renovating four months ago.

Proposing that he take the wild horses he bought at auction, gentling some for use on the ranch and some for Beau and Hank's new rodeo school, had changed Mitch from a ranch hand to a partner at the Double T. Not only did he have a stake in the ranch now, he'd moved out of the bunkhouse he'd lived in with the other hands and moved into the old foreman's house which was in bad need of repair. Mitch didn't care. He had his dreams. Being able to pocket the money from the sale of horses the Double T passed on made it possible for Mitch to buy his own spread sooner. That was his real dream.

Since Beau and Mandy had passed on Hank's offer to give them the foreman's house, instead opting to build their own home deeper into the ranch by the old creek, the house became his. He never minded the work of gutting it, hammering in new wallboard, room by room, because it was his home. At the end of a hard day, he went back to the solitude of stripping walls and pulling out whatever nonsalvagable wood and trim that remained.

But his home wasn't the same as it was four months ago. In fact, it was a far cry from anything he'd imagined. Things had changed. Drastically. Everything now revolved around a little boy who at the moment was as scared and disjointed as Mitch.

Now, instead of being able to work at his leisure, Mitch couldn't run power tools in the house if the baby was sleeping. And Sara seemed to bring color and life to his sparse decor with odds and ends she'd brought back with her from L.A.

"A child's mind is stimulated by color and music," she'd said when she asked if she could put up a few things to give the place some interest.

Mitch had to admit the place looked more inviting, not to mention lived-in. Since he'd always taken his meals with the rest of the hands at the main house, he didn't feel the need to fill his cabinets with too many dishes or glassware. Now his kitchen was filled to overflowing with breakables. Crystal and fancy china and vases.

He heard her singing softly when he walked through the door. She immediately stopped as soon as she saw him.

"Did you already have something to eat?" Mitch asked.

"No, I was waiting for you. Jonathan kept me busy and I wasn't able to get started until a little while ago," Sara said.

He peered down at the dinner already placed on the table between two place settings. "You made this for me?"

"It's going to be a few more months before Jonathan can eat steak and potatoes," she replied with a smile.

The table was set with white linen, embroidered napkins, and silverware that he knew hadn't come from his kitchen.

"These are different. Are they new?" he asked, picking up one of the napkins.

"No. More boxes arrived from L.A. today."

"More?"

She chuckled at the expression he'd made. "This is the last of it. I promise you. Are you sure you don't mind me putting these things out? You didn't have a table cloth and—"

"No, it looks nice."

She smiled her pleasure and he found his breath hitch in his throat. Was it always going to be like this? Sure, he found Sara attractive. Okay, he was attracted to the woman in a big way. He could admit it. But his palms didn't have to get all sweaty just because she was in the room. He didn't have to go dizzy just seeing her face light up with a smile.

"It was fun opening the boxes and taking out the china and fine linens. It made things seem real, you know? Like, 'I'm no longer in L.A., I'm home.' Feels kind of good."

"I guess that would bring it home, wouldn't it," he said lamely.

Miss Hollywood. That's what she was. She may have grown up on the reservation, but Sara had changed into a different woman than most of the girls he knew around these parts. There was a certain glamour about her that was striking. She appreciated fine things that money could buy.

Yeah, he liked nice things too, but that could come later when he got his business breeding and training horses up and running. He didn't care much about the frilly things most women enjoyed; he just liked the women. But since Jonathan's arrival, there hadn't been much opportunity to enjoy anyone but the woman with him right now. Somehow, that suited him just fine.

He took the time to wash up before they both sat down to eat. Steak and potatoes were a welcome sight and had his stomach making all kinds of noises. The first night Sara had cooked dinner, she'd made some fancy dish with squid that had a name he still couldn't get right, and an appetizer with uncooked fish. He was hungry and it tasted good enough, but he could tell she knew it wasn't his thing.

Tonight she'd grilled a steak and made mashed potatoes, a hearty meal. After that first night, he wasn't quite sure what to expect from someone who ate raw fish on a regular basis, but the steak and potatoes tasted like they always did.

Things were getting back to normal again, he thought with amusement.

The conversation during dinner was mostly small talk about her plans to open a preschool on the reservation and bring back the stories of her Apache culture. Mitch talked of his experience gentling horses and the changes in the ranch over the past year.

After dinner, when all he wanted to do was head out into the workshop to finish up Jonathan's crib, Sara instead shooed him out of the kitchen to take a shower and change so he could give Jonathan his nightly bottle-feeding. Mitch knew what she was doing, forcing this quality time thing. Bonding is what she'd called it.

Heck, that was fine. Jonathan was his son after all. But Mitch couldn't help his feelings no matter how many bottles of formula he fed the baby.

To Mitch, Jonathan still seemed so foreign. Still so strange, it scared him.

When he'd finished giving Jonathan his nightly bottle and the baby was deep into a formula-induced sleep, he set him in the cradle in Sara's room, paying particular care that he was propped up on his side as Sara instructed. Then he went downstairs, intending to go to the workshop, but found himself wandering into the kitchen. He found Sara there, seated at the table with a pile of baby clothes.

"You're getting better at it," Sara said, not looking up at him when he walked into the room.

He took a moment to look at her. Really look at her. Her hair was pulled back in a wide white headband that made a striking contrast to her almost-black hair and the gold hoop earrings she wore. Her silk blouse and flowing slacks billowed, hiding the slender curves he knew were there. She wore a pair of gold sandals.

For the first time, he realized he had never seen Sara in a pair of blue jeans. He was going to have to buy her a pair of cowboy boots just to keep her from killing herself walking around the ranch in those sandals.

"How can you tell?" he finally asked.

"You didn't call me once to come rescue you." She lifted her face to him then and he saw the slight tilt in her full lips. His head went into a cataclysmic spin and his heart hammered. How could one woman affect him so strongly?

"Maybe he's getting used to me."

"He's not the only one."

Mitch couldn't help but smile. He liked that about Sara. You never really wondered what she was thinking when you walked into the room. She'd let you know in her subtle way. It was a far cry from all the secrets Lillian had kept from him.

"What are you doing?" he asked as he opened the refrigerator and pulled out a pitcher of orange juice.

She kept her concentration on the clothes, cocking her head to one side as she placed one outfit on top of another, then discarding one only to do it all over again with another. When she decided on a piece, she started cutting it into a square.

"Jonathan doesn't fit in this outfit anymore," she said.

"Already?" He'd practically croaked out the word. "They haven't even been washed once."

She chuckled. "Twice, actually. Babies grow really fast at this age. I could change his outfit every time I change his diaper just to get some wear out of his clothes."

"So what are you doing with them?"

"I thought I'd start a quilt. I can cut squares out of the clothes that don't fit him anymore. It won't be long before I have enough fabric to finish it. Years from now you'll be able to look back on this quilt and picture him as he is now, so tiny and innocent. It'll help you keep your sanity when he's bent on destroying the place and getting into trouble like most young cowboys."

Mitch hooked his thumbs in the front pocket of his jeans and leaned against the counter. "Not my boy," he said, a bit of pride making him grin.

"Yeah, right," she retorted.

Miss Hollywood.

"What did you say?"

Sara was looking at him directly now, having abandoned the swatches of fabric she'd been intent on cutting and arranging when he walked into the room. Mitch hadn't realized he'd said the words aloud until Sara lifted her wide brown eyes at him, casting him a cautious, quizzical look.

"You're not like the girls from around here. You dress like a model out of some glamour magazine."

"Really? I hadn't seen any of those magazines lying around the house," she said dryly.

"All I need is eyes. And I have two very healthy ones."

"I'm sure."

"You're sitting there all fancy while you're cutting squares for a quilt. It's quite a contrast."

He'd upset her. Mitch could tell by the sudden tightness in her voice and the stiffness in her movement.

"Clothes are just the outer shell. There's much more to me."

"I'm sure there is. That's something I'd like to discover."

"That's not likely to happen."

He shook his head at his stupidity. "I offended you and I didn't mean to. I'm sorry about that. I just . . . hadn't pictured having a woman as beautiful as you in my home making a baby blanket for my kid."

"Backpedaling won't help."

"How about this, Sara? I find you very intriguing and I'd like to get to know you better."

She sighed, her eyes drifting back to the squares in her lap. "That's something you'll have to do without, Mr. Broader."

He quirked an eyebrow and straddled the chair next to where she sat at the table. "Now who's backpedaling? 'Mr. Broader' is awfully formal."

"You're my employer."

He chuckled. "Since when? You've been speaking your mind with me ever since you stepped foot on this ranch. Why put up a wall of etiquette now?"

She was silent for a few seconds. When she spoke, her voice was very quiet.

"It's easier that way."

"In some ways, maybe. When two people are strangers."

"We're strangers."

She looked at him then and he saw a glimpse of the fire in her he'd come to enjoy and he laughed.

"Not anymore. Everywhere I look I see you in this house and I've come to rely on you being here." More than he'd ever relied on anyone, he realized.

Sara lifted her chin just a bit. "Living under the same roof doesn't mean we know the intimate details of each other's life. We hardly know each other at all."

He nodded his agreement. There was a quietness about Sara when she spoke. Like nothing could ever really ruffle her feathers. He had the delicious feeling he'd like to try a little ruffling, just to see a little spark ignite, to see those dark brown eyes flash with some fire. But he suspected that was a rarity with a woman like her.

He quickly got up from the table when the kettle on the stove whistled, silencing it before it woke Jonathan. He'd be waking soon enough and right now Mitch was enjoying the quiet conversation.

Sara had set two mugs with tea bags on the counter before setting the kettle to boil. Mitch didn't drink tea, but to him it was an invitation. And he was going to accept it rather than put his foot in his mouth again. They'd spent nearly two weeks together in his house and knew as much about each other as the day she'd arrived.

He poured the cups of tea, dropped two spoons into the mugs and carried them over to the table.

"So why did you come back?"

Her expression pinched into a frown. "Out of everything you could ask about me, *that* is what you want to know?"

Mitch shrugged. "It's a place to start. I figure I have a good idea about why you left."

"You do?"

"Sure. I may not have known you from talking to you, but I've been here over ten years. I've known your mom the whole time."

"And mothers talk," she said with a soft groan.

"Did you think it was a secret?"

"I guess not."

"You don't have to tell me anything you don't want to."

"I don't really like to talk about myself all that much." Sara carefully folded the pieces of fabric she'd just cut and placed them in a basket on the table. She stared down at her tea and bobbed the tea bag up and down in silence.

"So, Lillian wanted something you weren't prepared to give?"

"How did this all of the sudden turn to Lillian?"

Sara eyed him wryly. "You didn't think you'd be the only one doing the discovering, did you?"

"Touché."

"It's natural for me to want to know about Jonathan's mother. When I look at him all I can think about was how hard it must have been for her to leave him here. What she must be thinking right now without him."

"You don't know Lillian. I'm surprised she even chose to have Jonathan."

Sara snapped her head toward him in surprise. "And that would have been easier on you, right?"

Mitch sighed. "That's not what I meant. I'm not doing very well at all explaining myself tonight. All I meant is knowing Lillian, I can't see her saddling herself with a kid. It doesn't really surprise me that she chose to leave him with me. And I keep thinking of what he'll feel when he grows up wondering why she left him."

"You'll tell him the truth."

Mitch took a sip of the tea and grimaced at the bitter flavor. "The truth isn't pretty."

"Do you even know the truth?"

As he reached for the sugar bowl on the table and started spooning sugar in his cup, he said, "I know enough."

Sara chuckled softly. "Mitch Broader, you're so all-fired sure of yourself."

"No, I'm not. You've seen firsthand how very unsure I am with Jonathan. I don't know how people have kids without feeling like complete imbeciles. How do these kids ever survive to adulthood with parents like me who don't have a clue? I mean, you need a license to drive a car, but you can have a kid without any instruction at all. All kids should come with manuals."

"No one is born a parent. It's a learning process." She gave him a crooked smile before sipping her tea, then said, "It's nice to hear you talking about him like that."

"Like what?"

"Your son. You're his parent. You've accepted it. I thought that wall you had up was going to stay there forever."

Mitch shrugged. What could he say? "It's not like I have a choice. He looks just like me."

"It's more than that and you know it. You're already falling in love."

Yeah, he was, Mitch realized. But Jonathan wasn't the only one who was stirring his feelings and twisting him into knots. Sara was doing a pretty good job of it herself.

"We were married. Lillian and I," Mitch said quietly. He didn't know why, but it was important for Sara to know this, even though it was something Mitch had vowed to strike from his memory. Some lessons were learned the hard way and his whirlwind relationship with Lillian definitely qualified as hard.

Sara seemed to shrink in her chair. "Oh. I just assumed."

"Yeah, I figured. It's not something I like to talk about much." He stole a glance at her, trying to read her expression, but came up empty.

"And Lillian didn't tell you she was pregnant?"

"There wasn't much time for that. The marriage lasted all of two weeks."

"Two whole weeks? You're not much for longevity, are you?"

Mitch winced. "Ouch. I had the marriage annulled when I came home early with roses in my hand after meeting with my grandfather's attorney, only to find another man's shoes parked where my boots should have been." That was something that had broadsided him pretty bad. He'd known Lillian since he was a kid, having grown up on the same block. They'd hung out together and even shared their first real kiss.

Sara's eyes drifted closed. "I'm sorry," she said quietly.

He gave an idle shrug. "I'm okay with it now."

"No, I mean I'm really sorry. For the . . . terrible things I was thinking about you. It wasn't my place to judge."

He sighed, his voice tight when he spoke. "You thought I ran out on Lillian, didn't you?"

She nodded apologetically. "It's so cliché and I shouldn't have assumed. Mandy never mentioned you were married."

"You talked to Mandy about me, huh?"

She tossed a baby bib at him and said dryly, "Don't go getting a big head. I told you I was curious about Jonathan's mother."

"Yeah," Mitch said, although he was unconvinced it was as simple as Sara was making it out.

"Her betrayal must have been quite a blow."

"It was a hard time for me with my grandfather sick and all. I'd known Lillian since I was a kid and well, I don't know, I needed a friend. Like me, she didn't have much as a kid, but she had her dreams. I don't think I would have been so blind to how Lillian had changed if I hadn't been so torn up with grief, knowing he was going to die. She's not the woman I knew growing up."

"I'm sorry."

"Thanks. It all happened way too fast," Mitch continued.

He couldn't believe he was talking about it, his marriage. That was something he'd never really done since the annulment. But Sara made it easy. Those warm, dark brown eyes wrapped around him, not in sympathy, but understanding.

"I'd gone back East when Grandpa was dying and met Lillian again. It was stupid of me to get into a relationship at such a bad time in my life, but I let the fact that we'd known each other once cloud my judgement. I needed something familiar. And after two weeks, we were talking marriage and making plans to head back to Texas."

"So Lillian has never lived on the ranch, then."

He shook his head just thinking about it. "We never got that far. It's probably why Mandy doesn't know anything about it. I told Hank about it. I figured he might have told Corrine, but I don't think it is common knowledge. It was one of those mistakes I figured was better left in the past."

He picked up the bib she'd tossed at him, thinking of the irony. He'd been crushed by her betrayal, but he thought at least she'd come to him, try to explain *something*. She'd let him go as easily as he'd walked away.

"When Lillian found out I wasn't going to inherit any of my grandfather's money, she decided 'till death do us part' was just a little too long for her. I didn't know anything about Jonathan until I walked into the house and found Corrine holding him."

He drained his tea and got up from the chair, scraping it against the floor as he pushed back from the table. As he set the empty mug in the sink, he tried to push away the pain of that period in his life.

"My grandfather was pretty much the one to save me from my parents."

"Save you?"

"I didn't have the best of childhoods. As marriages go, my parents' was pretty bad. Lot of yelling, slamming of doors and Dad wasn't always around.

"My parents were divorced when I was real young,

but neither one could let go of the other. My dad would run off for months at a time and mom always welcomed him back in. In between, she'd cry and when he was home . . . well, let's just say I raised myself in a lot of ways. It wasn't the perfect environment for a kid."

He'd learned to take care of himself, to hide if it meant escaping one of his old man's rampages. Sometimes Mrs. Santini, his next-door neighbor, would hear the fighting and sneak Mitch out of the house, give him a good meal and tuck him into bed at her house. His parents were never the wiser.

Mitch could still remember the way she rubbed his back as his tears fell. *No child should grow up this way*, she'd say.

Trust hadn't come easy for Mitch. That's why Lillian's betrayal stung as bad as it did, especially in light of Jonathan.

"Were they always like that?"

"As far back as I can remember." He thought about it a minute. He never liked talking about his past much. The happy times were too few, mixed in with all the bad.

And too quickly his own marriage spiraled into something too frighteningly close to what he'd known as a kid. The honeymoon was over before it even began and instead of loving each other, they'd spent those weeks fighting. Mostly over money. When he'd walked through the door that day and found Lillian with her "company," he saw himself as his father. And it scared him to death.

But instead of unleashing his anger the way he knew his old man would, Mitch had walked away, not even giving Lillian the opportunity to come to him and explain. She didn't protest either, which said a lot for the love they supposedly shared. He pushed those recent memories aside and thought of his childhood.

"My grandfather really tried to help my father but Dad was too concerned with a quick buck, an easy card game. He lost more than he won and spent whatever he did make on anything but his family. If I wanted something, my grandfather made me earn it. Even though he had some money, there were no free rides. He taught me a lot."

"Was he a rancher, too?"

"No, I never really knew what he did. He invested his money mostly."

She chuckled softly and he felt his heart swell with the musical sound. "Then how on earth did an Irish city boy from Baltimore become a cowboy?"

Mitch grinned and shrugged. "I was at the critical crossroads age where I could have easily slipped down the wrong path. I didn't trust anyone and was good at picking a fight because that's all I knew. Grandpa took me to a dude ranch the first few weeks I was here in Texas. And as miserable as I was to be away from home, he saw how much I loved being on that ranch. Something took hold of me. He told me if I worked hard, I could have one for my own one day. I could do anything I wanted to do as long as I didn't follow in my old man's footsteps."

"And you haven't."

It almost looked like pride shining in her eyes, Mitch thought. Warmth spread from deep in his chest outward until emotion lodged in his throat. He'd convinced himself early on in life he didn't need anyone.

His grandfather had taught him, even before he'd come to Texas to live with him, that he was strong and could accomplish anything he put his mind to. He needed to rely on himself to survive.

Having Sara gaze at him like that with those huge brown eyes filled with admiration touched a place in his soul he didn't even know existed.

The room suddenly seemed to crackle with tension. His eyes focused on her lips, the smooth planes of her cheeks.

Sara must have felt it too. She abruptly cleared her throat and looked at him teasingly.

"Well, Mr. Broader, since you've become a pro at feeding Jonathan his bottle, tomorrow we'll move on to changing his diaper."

"I just got used to holding him and giving him a bottle. The next thing you'll want is for me to give him a bath."

She tossed him a wicked grin. "That's the spirit."

Chapter Four

"How are you two doing in there?" Sara asked, trying her best to keep from plowing into the bathroom where Mitch was giving Jonathan his first bath solo. She paced the hallway, holding a clean diaper and sleeper to put the baby in after he was dried off, wanting nothing more than to march right in the bathroom and take over.

But she held herself back. After two nights of bathing Jonathan and insisting Mitch stand by and watch, Mitch had announced that "the boys" would give it a try on their own tonight so Sara could put her feet up and relax.

Fat chance of that, Sara thought, pacing the hallway. But she hadn't wanted to discourage Mitch when it was clear that things were going so well.

After their rocky start, Sara had hoped Mitch would open up and take Jonathan into his heart. For a while, Sara hadn't thought it was going to happen. But these past few days had changed dramatically. Both father and son had taken to each other as if they'd been together from the start.

Progress. That was very good. Unfortunately it left her feeling a bit disjointed about what to do with herself while she waited for success or disaster.

Put her feet up. Yeah, right!

She'd paced the hallway, only leaving to answer the telephone, which annoyingly enough, turned out to be two wrong numbers. She quickly bounded back to the hallway, pressing her ear to the door when things became too quiet for her peace of mind.

It wasn't working. Aside from looking like an idiot with her cheek pressed up against the freshly painted wood door, she was getting a stiff neck.

"You need any help in there?" she called out again when her first question was left unanswered.

There was a loud slosh of water and a quick, low, grunt that had Sara bursting through the bathroom door. She found Jonathan sitting upright and secure in his baby bathtub, a small rubber duck tub toy clutched between his chubby fingers.

"I'm okay," Mitch said, getting himself upright. "I just slipped on a little water."

"A little?" She glanced at the wet floor surrounding him. There was about a gallon of water on the floor and a gallon of water on Mitch. His dark hair was slick with wetness as was his faded jeans. Even though he'd cuffed the sleeves of his white button-down oxford shirt, that too was soaked.

"You didn't tell me you were going to take a bath with him," Sara teased, pulling a fresh towel from the linen closet and opening it up to receive the baby.

Mitch cocked his head to one side and pulled the baby from the tub. "Very funny. I think we did pretty good for a first time. Don't you think, buddy?"

Jonathan let out a squeal of glee and kicked his wet legs furiously as Mitch lifted him in the air to the waiting towel. Sara wrapped Jonathan in the towel and held him close. When she nuzzled his cheek, he rewarded her with the sweet smile that reminded her so much of his father.

"Give me a second to mop up this water and I'll get him dressed," Mitch said.

"It might take you more than a minute to clean this up. Why don't you let me give him his bottle and get him to bed? That way you can have some time in the workshop."

Mitch had mentioned at dinner that he was almost done making Jonathan's crib. He'd been spending little snatches of time in the workshop in between his ranch work, working with Beau on the final finishes to the barn and working the horses. It amazed Sara that there was time for Jonathan at all, and in truth, she feared Mitch would use his work at the ranch to keep himself distant. But he hadn't.

Mitch grabbed Jonathan's little fist and bending his head, gave it a gentle kiss. The warm emotion that instantly spread through her chest and lodged in her throat took Sara by surprise, but it was welcoming. Mitch's blue eyes were smiling when he finally glanced at her.

"Thank you, Sara," he said, quietly.

She left before she made a fool of herself by showing him just how much he'd affected her by doing something so simple and pure. Her heart racing, she grabbed the clean clothes she'd hastily discarded when she raced into the bathroom and headed upstairs to her room.

She had to stop this. It had been nearly a month since she'd come to the Double T and she feared her emotions were getting the best of her. The last time that had happened, she'd made the disastrous decision to leave home.

When Jonathan was finished with his nightly bottle, Sara tucked him in the cradle and closed the door. A creak in the stairs as she descended sounded loud compared to the soft music filtering in from the window. Mitch usually listened to music while he was out in the workshop.

Following the sound of the music, Sara walked outside, blotting out the small spot of spittle Jonathan had drooled on her shoulder with a dishrag as she went. Glancing at her shoulder, she grimaced. Spittle. How very attractive.

Usually when Mitch disappeared into the workshop, Sara left him alone. There wasn't any reason to disturb him and she had the feeling he relished the quiet after the sudden invasion on his privacy. Especially after she'd done her best to make sure he spent some "quality" time with his son.

An old '60s tune she recognized was playing on the radio. It was a far cry from the usual country and western music she heard around these parts and certainly a lot tamer than some of the new rock she'd had the occasion to sample in L.A. Every so often, in between verses, Mitch's voice would boom over the music on the radio.

She pushed through the wide cross-planked door of the workshop just in time to hear him belt out a chorus. She stifled the giggle that bubbled up her throat at the expression on his face when he saw that he'd been caught. Instead of shrinking with embarrassment, Mitch simply smiled a warm and friendly grin that welcomed her into his private place. It was the same unabashed, childlike smile that emerged from Jonathan.

"Gotta love the oldies."

"It's apparent you do."

He shrugged and kept right on applying polyurethane to the crib he'd been tirelessly working on in between ranch business and the horses. Along the side ends of the crib, Mitch had carved a cartoon design and smoothed out the edges. It was solid, yet delicate enough for his child to have sweet dreams in. At the top of each rail there were big, bright colored beads about the size of a half dollar that Jonathan could play with threaded through a sturdy piece of metal. The love and craftsmanship Mitch put into making the crib was evident. No wonder he was always so exhausted.

"It looks beautiful," she said, admiring all his hard work.

"If this coat takes well, it'll only need one more sanding and a final coat of clear. Then Jonathan can test it out."

"That's good. I don't know how much longer he can fit in that cradle."

Mitch smiled. Taking a soft white cloth and running

it around the rim of the can, he wiped off the excess clear liquid and tapped down the lid, sealing it tight. Carefully, as if he were holding his own child, he lifted the crib underneath a dry section and brought it over to another area of the workshop where it could sit undisturbed while the polyurethane set.

At a loss for words, Sara searched her mind for some subject that would qualify as meaningful conversation. She came up empty and decided anything would do. She'd forgotten that cowboys as a rule didn't say much until needed. They were much more comfortable with a companionable silence than the men she'd met in L.A., who always seemed to want to dominate the conversation with some sort of ego-boosting news.

But since she'd come to the ranch, she realized Mitch wasn't like that. He was quiet about himself, didn't offer any more than needed unless she asked. But he was open. There didn't seem to be any locked doors inside him. All she had to do was ask.

Unfortunately, the conversations they usually had revolved around Jonathan, which didn't leave any smooth openings to ask for more. Sara realized she definitely wanted to know something more about the man whose home she shared.

Mitch was the first one to speak.

"Never saw so much water flying in my life coming from one little baby."

Sara squashed down the vague disappointment that he'd chosen the standard topic that bound them. Recalling how she'd found them both in the bathroom with an ocean of water on Mitch and then more on the floor, she smiled. It had truly been a mess, but to Mitch's credit, he hadn't called her for help.

"He's a slippery little thing when he's wet."

"You did good," she praised.

They fell into silence again and Sara debated whether to leave him alone with his project or just watch him rearrange items in his shop.

She watched him. She loved his hands, wide and callused from work. Strong, capable hands that made a woman feel safe. Her heart seemed to flutter like the wings of a butterfly just thinking about what his hand would feel like on the small of her back while he moved her through a crowded room. Or on her face as he gazed at her with his deep blue eyes.

She'd seen him working in the barnyard, hauling bags of feed and hoisting spools of barbed wire onto the truck with ease. Years of working hard had given him strength, yet she knew firsthand how gentle he could be with Jonathan. Hands built for working. And for loving. He'd transferred that same love and care to his work here, crafting his son's bed.

Sara's ex-husband had his hands manicured religiously, as did she. A quick glance at her own nails now had her curling her fingers under self-consciously. They'd been neglected since she'd come to Steerage Rock. No longer was there the time to pamper herself with a routine that was rarely broken back in L.A., now that Jonathan took up so much of her time.

Not ready to face the quiet of the house, Sara stayed and watched Mitch. His dark brown hair was getting a little too long in the front and a lock of hair kept draping across his startling blue eyes. With a quick swipe of his hand that she could swear he was barely aware of, Mitch pushed the hair aside while keeping his mind concentrated on his work.

Dedication. Love. It was both, she decided.

You needed dedication and love to dig in roots.

She'd come out here to ask him a question, but as she heard the DJ come back from a commercial and spin another classic, she settled back against the workbench and listened. Every so often, Mitch would start singing.

She was smiling when he finally glanced at her.

"What? Did I do something wrong?"

Shaking her head, she said, "You were born in the wrong decade."

"Nah. You forget I'm not from around these parts. When I was a kid, me and my friends listened to Motown and classic rock. It was considered classic from the '60s and '70s even then, but we couldn't get enough of it."

He danced around, tools in hand, singing and smiling as if he were doing it for her entertainment. And maybe he was. He seemed to take pleasure in her laughter.

"Oh, this is one of my favorite songs," he said, turning the radio up loud enough so the booming bass bounced off the walls of the workshop. He came toward her with arms stretched open wide.

"Mitch, I won't be able to hear the baby."

"He won't wake up. Besides, it's just a short song. Come dance with me, Sara."

Her pulse jackhammered. Taking in his outstretched arms and the thought of having them wrapped around her, she shook her head, crossing her arms across her chest. "I'll pass. I think you're doing fine for the both of us."

"Ah, come on. Just one dance. The song is half over anyway."

Before she could stop him, he had her on her feet and in his arms, breezing her around the workshop floor like she was dancing on air. Her heart beat strong, like a timpani keeping time to the music.

Laughing, she let herself be taken by him. It had been a long time since she'd laughed so hard or let her guard down enough to have a little fun. Part of her, some hidden place deep inside her head, told her that it wasn't a good idea. But Sara ignored it.

Her stomach hurt from laughing so much, and her head was spinning like a record on a turntable. When the song ended, she tried to pull free, but Mitch held her tight.

"You're not getting away from me that easy," he said, his eyes dark, reflecting the wild desire she felt deep inside her.

A flutter of panic raced through her. What she was thinking, what she wanted, couldn't happen. When Mitch gazed at her this way, eyes an endless sea of warmth and charm, with arms so strong they made all the mistakes of the past melt away like ice on hot plate, her mind turned to mush. She couldn't think at all.

Sara wanted Mitch to kiss her, to feel that connection of man and woman. Her mind told her that it was only because they were two normal healthy adults, living together in the same house. It had nothing to do with real attraction and desire. But even that she knew was a lie. She was fiercely attracted to Mitch, and denying it didn't make it go away.

Wrapping his arms around her waist, Mitch drew Sara toward him as if they were going to dance a very intimate slow number. The music had somehow faded into the background and all she could hear was her own heart hammering in her chest, beating in time with Mitch's.

Sara focused on his lips and wondered what it would be like to be kissed by Mitch Broader. It was a dangerous thought, frightening, and yet, very exhilarating at the same time.

Mitch bent his head and brushed his lips against hers, sending shock waves pulsing through her veins. It was sweet, she realized, controlled in a way that she didn't feel. In a way that had her body begging for more. As he pulled back, his eyes flashed with a smoky passion. Sara realized how much strength he had to keep from losing control.

Vaguely disappointed that the music had started again, she let him twirl her around the dusty floor.

Mitch held her like a flower that would bruise if he applied the smallest amount of pressure. Yet his strength was evident in the way he moved her with him, leading, yet not demanding she go his way.

He winked once, and then, with his arm around her waist, dipped her back so he hovered above her and she had to cling to him to keep from falling.

She laughed at the sheer craziness of dancing in the workshop with Mitch. He laughed too. A rich sound that seemed to rumble deep inside him and match the magnetism that she was caught in. How did he do it?

The lyrics had ended and the music was winding

down. Mitch lifted her hand high in the air and twirled her around. By her own clumsiness, her hip caught a hammer sticking out from the workbench and pitched it, along with a small box of tool bits, over the edge. In the corner of her eye, Sara saw the movement, her mind anticipating the crash to the floor. What she didn't anticipate was Mitch's quick movement to catch the box of tools before it tumbled and hit the ground.

A stark image flashed in her mind, vivid and blinding, and suddenly she was no longer in the workshop, but in her kitchen in California. The face she saw coming at her wasn't Mitch's, but that of her ex-husband. With his quick movement toward her, Sara's breath caught in her throat and her arms flew up to her side, her fists bunching. Before she could register that she was not in L.A., but on the Double T Ranch, she scurried away to the far side of the workshop like a cat who'd been scared by the toppled box.

"Sara?"

As her rampant heartbeat slowed to a semi-normal pace, she saw Mitch was staring at her, his blue eyes wide and full of questions. His gaze swept from her face, to her trembling hands. It didn't take much to know Mitch was confused by her reaction.

It was all too much. Humiliation washed over her like a tidal wave, coupled with a need to explain that her reaction had absolutely nothing to do with him. It was her. All her. What she wouldn't do to turn back the clock and be in Mitch's arms again, surrounded by his strength. But it was just too much.

His handsome face pinched into a questioning frown. "It was just a box of tools."

"I know," she said in some faraway voice. *It was only a box of tools.*

She ran from the workshop without another word.

What the heck had just happened? Mitch couldn't figure it out. One minute he was holding Sara in his arms, his head feeling as light as a feather, the next she was running from him as if she were afraid he'd . . .

His gut coiled tight like a snake squeezing the life out of him, making it hard for him to breathe. Closing his eyes hard, he tried to even his breathing to keep from unleashing the sudden burst of anger consuming him. He took the time to cool down by gathering the disheveled tools now scattered all over the workshop floor.

As he picked up each bit and tossed it into the cardboard box, Mitch ached to go to Sara and pull her into his arms. Stop her trembling and erase that horribly frightened look from her eyes. He knew that look. He'd seen in on his own mother often enough to know what it meant.

But if what he was thinking were true, Sara wouldn't welcome him coming after her for answers or anything else. Still, he needed to know she was all right.

A short time later, he found her in the kitchen, standing at the sink clutching a dishtowel and drying dishes that already looked air-dried.

"Sara?"

She stilled, but didn't turn to look at him. He walked over to the cabinet right where she stood and reached up for a glass, placing it on the counter. She stiffened. And his gut clenched.

He wanted to comfort her, to touch her and tell her everything was all right. He brought his hand mere inches from her back and held it there, afraid of what reaction she might have to his touch. Then he pulled it stiffly by his side.

"I'd never hurt you, Sara," he whispered. "I don't want you to ever fear me like that."

"I don't," she replied quietly. It reminded him much too much of himself when he was a child.

"Okay." He sighed as he walked to the door, abandoning the glass of water he'd intended to have. "I'm going to go down to the corral to work the horses for while before it gets too dark."

Sara simply nodded. He waited by the door until she turned to look at him. Her rich brown eyes were wide and glassy, and she nodded again.

As Mitch lumbered to the corral, he called her ex-husband every despicable name he could think of. And himself the same for making Sara feel that vulnerable again.

From the kitchen window, Sara watched Mitch stroll out to the corral in a stride that was much more carefree than he must have felt. Especially after that episode in the workshop.

They were tools! Lousy tools that fell to the floor.

But as soon as Mitch came at her, it was as if she were in L.A. again, feeling all the fear and humiliation she'd felt whenever Dave came at her.

Her ex-husband had never struck her physically, although she could imagine him resorting to such measures. He claimed he was too refined for that. Instead, he used intimidation to keep her where he wanted her. His words stung and ate at the very marrow of her soul, depleting any confidence she had in herself.

In the beginning, it had been easy to go along with him. Dave was ten years older and seemed so worldly compared to how she felt. He'd told her how to dress to be sexy, what to say at parties to help him get promotions, who to be friends with to further their position in the community. They dined with Dave's colleagues every Friday night at the most exclusive restaurants in the city. The life he gave her in L.A. was something out of a glamorous Hollywood movie. And she wanted so much to fit in.

For a long time, she did. So Sara had allowed him take the lead. That was her biggest mistake.

Dave's wife would never work. It would mean that he couldn't provide a suitable home if she felt the need to have a job. After years of playing tennis and having superficial lunches with people who had nothing to talk about but vacationing in Europe or remodeling yet another section of their house, Sara decided she needed more. Volunteering at the daycare had been a compromise only after endless arguments.

It was there, as she sat with the children telling the Native American stories she'd been told as a child, that Sara's world had changed. The piece of herself she'd thrown away to be with Dave reemerged among the children, filling a gap that had grown wider with the years.

It was only then that Sara realized the façade her life had been. Friends she thought cared for her didn't want to hear about her heartache or what went on behind the closed doors of her apparantly perfect home. Sara learned to keep her mouth shut if she didn't want to be on the bad side of Dave's temper.

She'd become her husband's personal rag doll. Her cheeks flamed with shame even now, months after their divorce was final, to think of how she'd allowed him to manipulate her.

Mandy's surprise visit to L.A. had been a miracle. She recalled the humiliation she felt when Dave had come home and found the two of them laughing in the living room over bowls of Heavenly Hash ice cream. On the outside, she seemed strong and confident and had learned to assert herself. As long as Dave wasn't around. And as soon as he'd come home and done a once-over look at Mandy, Sara had turned inward again.

Ashamed at her own reaction and what she'd become, she'd given Mandy the excuse that she had a migraine and needed to lie down. Mandy had called her the next day to check on her. Sara had let the answering machine pick up the call and because of that, Mandy dropped by before heading to the airport on her way back to Texas.

"You have family and friends who love you in Texas," Mandy had said, looking past all the excuses Sara had given her. She'd hugged her fiercely at the door. "I'm not letting go of this friendship."

It had been the beginning of the end of her marriage, although in looking back, it had never been much of a marriage at all. Even though Sara hadn't been ready to leave L.A., Sara held on to Mandy's words and knew that she'd have the strength to leave eventually. And when she finally did have the courage to leave, there'd been no visible wounds for anyone to see.

But the scars were there, deep down, and one of them reared its ugly head at her tonight in front of Mitch.

She let out a heavy sigh and felt tears stinging her eyes once again. She could only imagine what Mitch must be thinking.

The sun was deep in the west when she climbed the stairs and checked on Jonathan. The bedroom was filled with a golden hue of burnt orange and red. Heat hung heavy in the air, but the baby seemed content enough sleeping in a cool cotton sleeper that fit snugly. Turning the baby monitor on, she grabbed the speaker and tucked it into the pocket of her light linen jacket.

She had to talk to Mitch and explain her reaction. The last thing she wanted was for him to think he'd done something wrong.

Midnight, the new mare Mitch had been working, was dancing rings around Mitch as he stood in the center of the corral. The light evening breeze coming in over the pasture was soothing. Sara pushed up the sleeves of her jacket to mid-arm and then hugged her middle as she approached the corral.

Nerves skittered through her veins as she absorbed the distance. Mitch isn't Dave, she reminded herself. No two men were more different. She had nothing to fear with Mitch.

Marveling at the power of his gentle touch with the horse, she watched for a few minutes, not wanting to break the spell. For days Sara had watched Mitch work his magic with Midnight. In the beginning, the mare had wanted no part of being bound in a corral. Mitch approached and Midnight ran away. But Mitch didn't give up.

The other day she and Mandy had sat beneath the cottonwood tree in front of the main house while Jonathan napped on a blanket. After Mandy had returned home, Sara's attention had been drawn to the corral. For a long time all she could do was watch Mitch and Midnight. When it seemed as if Midnight would never give an inch, she did, and the smooth, gentle strokes Mitch gave her in reward made tears spring to Sara's eyes.

He'd made great strides since then. Now, even as skittish as Midnight was, Sara could see the difference, the growing of trust. She almost envied it.

Still dancing in circles, Midnight eyed Mitch, seemingly aware of his every move. Mitch turned his back to the mare and played with the bridle, as if ignoring the horse. Finally, Midnight stopped running and with cautious steps, she moved forward, stopping every so often and taking a side step, bobbing her head or giving a neigh, as if calling Mitch to pay attention. Eventually, she stepped up alongside him and gave him one quick nudge with her nose, then another until she was settled beside him.

Ever so softly, Mitch stroked her head, neck, and front legs with long, easy strokes. He smiled his pleasure and crooned softly.

Without even realizing how he'd done it, Mitch got the bit in Midnight's mouth and the bridle around her head. He let the reins fall and allowed Midnight to get used to the bit.

Such trust, Sara thought.

"That's amazing," she said quietly. She felt like an intruder and, losing her nerve, turned to leave.

"Not really," Mitch said, glancing up at her as he kept his attention on the mare. He was looking at her as he had in the kitchen. Questions filled his eyes. "She still could bolt at any time."

Sara gripped the splintered rail of the corral. "But she hasn't. She came to you when she could have easily just kept running in circles."

"Trust isn't an easy thing for her. She still doesn't know what to think."

"She let you put the bridle on her. You didn't have to chase her. She came to you."

"I have to win her trust. And when I have it, I can't abuse it or she'll never give it up again."

Mitch carefully took the bridle off Midnight and took a few steps away. Midnight followed like a stray dog. *Incredible.*

"Does she trust you now? Enough to ride her?"

With his head low, Mitch shook his head. "We still need a little time together before she'll allow me put a saddle on her. Right now, she's letting me know her boundaries."

"She let you put a bridle on her as if she didn't even know you were doing it."

He chuckled and glanced up at Sara, his face bright with a smile. "Oh, she knew. But she's still making up her mind. She wants to trust me. I can tell. And maybe one day she will."

"Mitch?"

He looked up at her again from across the corral. He was incredibly handsome. His dark hair was the color of mica in the fading light and his eyes had turned from blue to a smoky gray. He stood tall, his weight shifted to one hip as he held the reins of the bridle.

Such strength.

Sara remembered all too well how it had felt earlier to be in Mitch's arms. Her heart still raced with the memory.

"What if she's never ready to trust you?"

Mitch's expression grew serious, pulling her into his gaze. He took a few steps closer, his boots kicking up dust from the ground as he walked. He stopped a good ten feet from where she was standing and said, "I can wait as long as it takes, Sara."

Chapter Five

"I'm leaving."

A jolt of panic hit Mitch square in the center of his chest like an electric shock. If he hadn't held tight to his spoon he would have dropped it in his corn flakes.

"Wha—why?" His eyes darted to the packed bags Sara carefully placed on the floor by the kitchen door. "I thought everything was going okay."

Sara's lips lifted ever so slightly at the corners. Her dark eyes deepened with a mixture of amusement and bewilderment. "What on earth are you talking about?"

"Me? What are *you* talking about? You just said you're leaving."

Her lips now curled into a full-blown smile and the spoon finally slipped from his fingers and plopped into the bowl of milk directly below.

"You didn't hear a word I said last night, did you, Mitch?"

Last night? He thought back to the night before and drew a blank. They'd talked briefly during dinner. And even then neither of them said much because Jonathan fussed and Sara kept getting up from the table to soothe him. She'd said he was cutting teeth and would probably be a little cranky for a while until they broke through his gums. After dinner, she'd spent some time rocking him to sleep.

Mitch had welcomed the reprieve. Things had been a little tense between them since the incident in the workshop. They talked amiably, mostly about Jonathan. Beyond that, he'd just been too busy for either of them to have time to talk about much else, let alone get past the awkwardness they'd felt since the night in the workshop.

He'd kissed her. He could almost taste her lips, the soft sweetness of her as he held her in his arms. Yeah, that had been a really swell idea, especially in light of what he'd suspected had gone on in her marriage. She had to have thought about it a thousand times since then, just as he had, and finally decided it was time to pack her bags.

But no, there was something else. Mitch searched the events of last night again and drew another blank. He'd been so tired lately that his mind was a bit foggy.

"What did we talk about?" he finally asked, admitting defeat.

"My taking Jonathan to the reservation today. It's Mom's day off and I thought I'd go do a little investigating, maybe even connect with an old friend or two so I can plan out the next few months. I want to meet with the school principal and see about setting up some storytelling classes in the curriculum. Mom said she'd watch Jonathan while I did all that."

It sounded vaguely familiar. He'd been working the horses more and more lately, pleased with the progress he'd made with them. He'd gone straight to the corral after dinner. After that he'd gone into the workshop to finish the final touches on the baby's crib. He'd been so tired when he walked upstairs that he'd gone straight to bed and slept like a dead horse.

No, he'd met Sara in the hallway for just a brief moment before he'd turned in. That must have been when she'd mentioned her plans.

Mitch shrugged apologetically. "Yesterday was a really long day." He nodded to the overnight bag. "What's that for?"

"I have some things, some presents to give my family. It was easier to stuff them all in a suitcase with the things Jonathan was going to need than to carry everything loose."

He nodded his understanding.

"You look relieved."

Mitch gave a quick laugh and settled back in his chair, wiping the spilled milk with a paper towel. "I am. I thought you were leaving. For good."

Abruptly, Sara's expression changed and Mitch didn't want to go where he knew this conversation was going to take them.

"I'm going home eventually, Mitch. I thought you understood that when I agreed to help you take care of Jonathan."

"I know. You did." Not that they talked about it

much or that he liked the idea. But Sara had made her intentions clear.

"Have you had any luck finding a replacement for me?"

"No." He wasn't being fair, he knew. He hadn't even begun looking for another nanny. When did he have time? Besides, no one would be able to live up to his expectations after Sara.

He needed her. He *wanted* her. In more ways than he cared to admit at the moment.

"Would you like me to ask around? People on the rez are always looking for good jobs. Mom might know a few girls that may be interested."

His head jerked to her and he saw immediate alarm sharpen her features. She quickly pulled a chair away from the table and sat down next to him.

"I wouldn't make any offers of employment. Anyone I thought was right for the job I'd merely ask to see you here. You'd be able to meet them and make your own decision about who is a right fit for you and Jonathan."

You're the right fit for us, Sara. He didn't say the words, knowing he'd be completely backing out of their arrangement if he did.

Truth is, he didn't want someone else moving into his house. Someone with different ways, different likes and dislikes different pictures to hang on the wall. It was hard enough for him to admit he needed Sara. He'd finally gotten used to the idea and now she was talking about leaving. Sure, she'd always talked about her plans of being a storyteller. But somehow, he couldn't imagine her really leaving him. *Them*, he corrected himself silently.

"I just figured I could make it easy by helping you since you have so little time."

"Sure," he said, a little harsher than he intended.

He walked to the refrigerator and yanked open the door. A pitcher of formula was already made and chilling. He had to move it to reach the milk.

She glanced at the cereal bowl on the table. "Do you want something else to eat? A bowl of cereal is not that much."

"You don't have to feed me. I can take care of myself."

Sara looked at him thoughtfully, lingering to see what emotion was behind this sudden coolness that had filled the air around them. "I know I don't have to. Pass me the pitcher of formula, please?"

He did so, and grabbed the carton of milk for himself.

"Since I obviously missed our conversation last night, why don't you fill me in? Are you going to be gone the whole day?"

"I made you a lunch."

His shoulders sagged slightly. "That's not why I'm asking."

She was going to find a *replacement*. Mitch knew it was coming. He'd known all along this was just a temporary arrangement. But the thought of having someone else here in Sara's place just didn't sit well with him. He glanced around the kitchen. She'd be gone and everything about her would go with her. He didn't like that thought. He only hoped that her sudden push to leave wasn't because he'd been an idiot the other night and kissed her.

"I suspect most of the day. I'll probably be back later this evening, if you don't mind."

He simply nodded. Why would he mind? It was the first time in a long time he'd have his house to himself again. No crying. No cares about waking up the baby.

"Is that a problem?" she asked when he didn't respond.

He glanced at her then and realized his mind had drifted.

"No, in fact it may work out nice. I can paint the walls in Jonathan's bedroom and set up the crib. Get it ready to move him out of your room."

She smiled. "There's no rush. It's easier to have him in the room with me until he's sleeping through the night."

"A new nanny might want her own room."

Her expression was unreadable. After a short pause, she gave a quick nod and went about filling bottles with formula for the day.

Jonathan started to cry and Sara quickly abandoned the bottles to tend to his son. Mitch closed his eyes and silently gave himself a hard word or two. What he'd done hadn't been fair to Sara. She hadn't lied to him or led him on. He was the one who had changed the plan. He wanted things to stay exactly the way they were. But sooner or later they *would* change. After his charming mood today, she just might make certain it was sooner rather than later.

Sara reached down and scooped Jonathan up from his cradle into her arms. She loved the feel of him, the way he smelled and the way his face suddenly transformed when his eyes caught sight of her or Mitch.

Mitch had given her the cold shoulder about going to the reservation today. She wasn't sure exactly what was bothering him. Whether it was because of her offer to help look for her replacement or that she was taking Jonathan away from the ranch for the day, she wasn't sure.

Part of her hoped it was the latter. He'd bonded somewhat with his son, but Sara could tell that there was a wall there, carefully kept in check as if he were waiting for Lillian to come back and tell him that it had all been a lie, that Jonathan wasn't really his son at all. Or maybe because he had every intention of tracking Lillian down and giving Jonathan back. Whatever the reason, Mitch was keeping a careful distance.

But none of that was any of her business. She'd told Mitch she was only going to stay until someone permanent could be found. She had her plans to move back to the reservation and teach the stories of her culture to the children. Nothing had changed. She glanced down at the now fully awake Jonathan, who was grinning up at her with a drooly, toothless grin.

Her heart squeezed. This had changed, as she knew it would. She nuzzled the baby's neck until he let out a high-pitch squeal of delight. She was becoming very attached to this beautiful baby. He wasn't just a child that she visited at the daycare and then handed over to the arms of its mother. This child looked up at her with the innate trust reserved for a parent, a primary person in his life.

Except, she wasn't Jonathan's mother. She wasn't a permanent part of his life or Mitch's. Soon she would leave. Her heart gave another tug of pain and longing.

She should make it soon.

"It's beautiful, Mother," Sara said, holding the blue and white dress up for view. The tiny metal "fringes" that had been sown all the way around the jingle dress sounded like rain as she moved.

"I knew you'd like it," Alice said, her face beaming with delight. "A little over a year ago, after Mandy came back to Texas, I had a dream that you were wearing it."

Sara tried not to show her shock. The jingle dress was used by Native American women to dance at the powwow. Many stories were told of a sick child who needed healing. Her grandfather had a dream that she was wearing a beautiful, colorful dress that jingled as she moved, making music. The child had been healed.

"Me? But Mother, I don't need to be healed."

Her mother eyed her knowingly. "Are you sure, sweetheart?"

"I've visited my doctor in L.A. before I left and I'm as fit as can be," she said, knowing full well her mother wasn't talking about her health.

"You're still so unsure of your step."

"I'm getting steadier on my feet," Sara quickly insisted. "It's been a long time since I've been back to the rez. L.A. is so different, the people, the environment, the pace. It's taking a while to slow down and really feel like I'm home."

"It's not home that hurt you." Alice wrapped her hands about Sara's as she held the dress to her chest. "He hurt you, didn't he?"

Sara hesitated. What mother wanted to hear such horrors? And yet, to deny what went on in her life back in L.A. would have been wrong.

"Never with his hands," she replied truthfully.

"But with his words."

"Yes," she admitted softly.

"Then it's your heart that needs healing so you can trust again. So you can begin to love again."

Sara chuckled wryly and carefully set the dress down over the basket her mother had retrieved it from. It was delicate and needed to be handled with the care and love with which it was made. There was a time, many years ago, when she wouldn't have appreciated the beauty of such a dress, when she would have balked at its meaning.

"I'm done with all that, Mother."

A quick laugh came from deep in Alice's throat and escaped her lips. "I've lived a lot more years than you, child. I see the way you look at him. I can see love when it's there."

Her head snapped up to meet her mother's gaze, her mouth agape. "It's not like that."

Her mother offered a wry smirk. "The heart listens to no one. Even the sensible mind that tells it something different."

She forced words past the sudden lump that lodged deep in her throat. "I'm not ready to go through that again."

"And what was that?"

Tears that seemed to come from deep in her soul welled up in her eyes. "I'm not ready to talk about it, either."

"You're not the same woman you were before.

Deep down you're the same Sara that left the reservation, but the woman who has come home is changed. You're stronger," Alice said.

"Yes, I am," she said quietly, trying her best to give her mother a smile of reassurance. Trying, too, to feel the confidence of making such an achievement. "But I still can't talk about it."

Alice pulled her daughter into a tight embrace. "Then you can dance at the powwow. When you're ready to talk, I'm here."

The day had both good points and bad points. On a somewhat positive side, the school administration was excited about the prospect of adding a storytelling class to the curriculum, but encouraged Sara to move beyond Steerage Rock to teach the Apache history to Native American children who no longer lived on the reservation. It wasn't exactly what she'd thought of herself doing, being off the reservation, but it made sense to reach those who didn't have the benefit of living the culture firsthand.

And despite good intentions, Sara's efforts for finding someone who was willing to work as Jonathan's nanny were futile. Oh, there had been many interested parties. But most involved simply day care instead of living on the premises, which of course she knew Mitch really wanted and needed given the disjointed hours he worked on the ranch. He needed someone round the clock so he could leave the house on a moment's notice. Many of the young girls who were would-be candidates either weren't ready for the responsibility or didn't want the commitment of something so isolating.

Sara understood that as much as she understood her

own need to find someone to replace her quickly. Not only so she could begin her work as a storyteller, but because of her visit with her mother. *Especially* in light of her visit with her mother.

Her heart needed healing. That much Sara couldn't deny. But not so that she could move on to love Mitch. It just couldn't happen. And the sooner she found a replacement and left the Double T and Mitch's home, the better off they'd all be.

The headlights of the car bobbed up and down the Double T driveway. A sense of calm washed over her to be heading home again. *Home*. Now where had that come from? The Double T was not her home. Her home was on the reservation.

Jonathan murmured in his sleep and she glanced in the mirror to check on him in the backseat where he slept in his car seat.

Pulling up in front of the foreman's house that Mitch occupied, she realized this wasn't her home either. Why on earth had she thought of that?

He needed to know the truth. Deep down, Sara knew Mitch thought of her as his salvation in a situation that was thrust upon him. But she wasn't anyone's salvation, least of all this cowboy's.

They'd need to talk. And it needed to be soon.

It was time he learned the real truth about Sara Lightfoot.

Sara found Mitch in the bedroom, folding up old drop cloths that had been spattered with sky-blue paint. The bedroom smelled thickly of paint and the open window did little to air it out.

She knocked on the door when he didn't turn around.

Mitch turned with a start. "I didn't hear you drive up."

"We just got back."

"Did you have a good time?" He wiped his hands on the thighs of his paint-splattered jeans, and reached for Jonathan.

"I don't think it'll take much for him to fall asleep. He didn't have much of a nap since there were so many kids and so many arms to pass him to at my mother's."

Mitch took Jonathan in his arms and gave him a kiss on his head. Jonathan shifted and fussed but Mitch didn't seem uncomfortable with it. The warmth in his eyes showed he was genuinely happy that they were home.

"If you don't mind," Mitch said, handing the baby back to Sara. "I'd like to change my clothes and give him his bottle before putting him down."

Sara nodded, a slight tug pulling at her heartstrings. "That would be good. It'll give me a few minutes to unpack things and straighten up. I'll get his bottle ready."

She turned to leave but then stopped, turning back to Mitch. "It you're not too tired I'd like to talk later."

"Sure," he said, his face still holding all the joy at seeing them. Or rather, seeing his son. "I'll meet you downstairs in a little while."

Mitch held Jonathan in his arms for a lingering second before bending his head to give his son a kiss on his forehead. The baby smelled clean and sweet with fresh baby powder. Sara had sponge-bathed Jonathan while Mitch was taking a shower, scrubbing off all the pale blue paint that had splattered on his hands and face while he painted Jonathan's bedroom.

Sara wanted to talk, she'd said. That could mean only one thing. She found a replacement.

Mitch didn't really want to think about it. And he certainly didn't want to talk about it. He just wanted Sara to stay. He couldn't imagine another woman in his home. But it was looking as if the choice wasn't his to make.

He placed the baby in his cradle, marveling at how big he'd grown in just a few short weeks he'd been here in Texas. Things had changed so drastically. If Mitch was honest with himself he'd have to admit that this change was good. In some ways anyway. He'd gotten used to taking care himself. He didn't have many friends but the friends he did have were solid.

Yeah, life had gotten a little complicated with a kid and a woman living under his roof. But he had gotten used to it. It had surprised him today when he found himself missing them as he was painting the bedroom.

And now Sara was going to up and leave him.

He took his time walking downstairs and found Sara sitting in the living room, the lights dim. He wasn't ready for this conversation. There was no sense being a coward when he knew the inevitable was coming.

"I'll bet he's already asleep," she said, lifting those incredibly warm brown eyes to meet his.

She knew Jonathan so well. Mitch deposited the nearly empty bottle on the end table and sat down next to her on the couch.

"He didn't drain his bottle. And that's a lot for this little muncher."

Sara smiled one of those sweet smiles that always seem to make his head spin and his heart thump louder in his chest.

"I take it today went well then?"

"Not as well as I hoped, I'm afraid," she said with a shrug. "I did a little digging and unfortunately I wasn't able to come up with one solid name to give you as a replacement for me."

He felt tension drain from his muscles for the first time since this morning, when Sara had announced she would start looking for a nanny on her own. The knot in his shoulders suddenly released. Leaning back in the sofa, he stretched his arm out over the back, wanting so much to touch Sara, stroke her smooth-as-silk cheek with his fingers, knowing without a doubt he absolutely shouldn't. It had been a long day for both of them. He could see the pull of fatigue in her dark eyes, yet they were so beautifully sweet all the same.

"I asked my mother to check with a few more people." She shook her head. "But they're all so young. I'm afraid they're just not up to handling how active Jonathan can be."

Mitch chuckled and threw her a smile. "He's just a baby, not even walking yet."

"But he will be." Sara chuckled herself. "And believe me when he does he's not going to walk. That child is going to run."

"He's just like his old man."

He knew he shouldn't do it, but he spoke his mind. After all, Sara had done plenty of speaking her mind.

It was one of the things he truly admired about her. "Guess you're just going to have to stay then."

Her laughter vanished, but Mitch didn't regret revealing what he felt. He wanted Sara to stay. And he wanted her to know exactly how he felt about it.

"I made plans to start teaching some classes at the elementary school in about a month. My mother offered to watch Jonathan if I don't have a replacement by then."

Mitch sighed, not bothering to hide his disappointment. "That's good," he said. The last thing he wanted was to make her feel she *had* to stay. Sure, he wanted her to stay. But that's because he liked her. Okay, it was much more than that. He could admit it, at least to himself. These feelings that were swirling around inside of him, at times making him insane with thinking about her, had become a major distraction. A sweet distraction.

Sara forced a smile. "It's a start. It wasn't exactly what I was hoping for. But I do agree with the administration. Children on the reservation get a certain amount of the culture just by being here and living their life here. Even if they balk at it. They hear the stories from the cradle. The Native American children living off the reservation don't ever get exposed to the culture. Those are the children I should be trying to reach. I hadn't really thought about it until today. But there is a program I can start at the daycare level a day or two a week. And that should keep me busy for a while."

Mitch refused to feel hopeful. It didn't mean anything, only that Sara wasn't leaving today. She was still looking for a replacement to watch Jonathan.

"I've done a lot of thinking, looking at myself. And some of it was hard to look at."

"What are you talking about?"

"You asked me why I came back to Texas. That's not really as important as why I left. You said you had a pretty good idea of why I left. But I don't think you really do."

"Why don't you tell me, then?" he asked.

"I'm only part Apache," she responded carefully.

"I remember Alice telling me that."

"When I was really young it didn't make a difference. I didn't really know what I didn't have outside the reservation. But as I got older I began to see other girls, girls that weren't Native American. I began to get, well, jealous."

She was clearly uncomfortable with what she was telling him, although Mitch couldn't figure out why. "That makes you the average American teenager."

"It was more than that. It wasn't just simply wanting a dress that some other girl had. Those girls were different. Life on the reservation is so different than living off it. And then I met Dave."

She fiddled with her fingers in her lap and averted her gaze. "I was only seventeen at the time. I'd been coming to the Double T to visit Mandy during the summer while Mom worked. But then she stopped coming." She shook her head and let out another sigh. "I'm ashamed to say that I was actually jealous of Mandy. She was—is—a great friend. She seemed to have it all. She told me all about Philadelphia and people she knew there and what she and her friends did. I didn't have any of that. I blamed it on being Native American."

Mitch remained silent. There wasn't anything shocking in which she was saying. Lord, if she had a taste of his past she would know that none of this matter now. What was important was who she was now.

"Dave was older. I think of it now, and I was truly stupid. He had gone to college in Dallas, although he'd graduated some years before. He'd been out in the workforce for a few years and was now starting to make some serious money. Liked spending on me." She gave her shoulder and idle shrug. "I liked him spending it on me."

Her voice was so quiet, so small. She sat on the opposite side of the couch just staring at him with eyes so wide it almost frightened her.

"He talked about L.A. and I would just sit there mesmerized, like he was living one of those Hollywood movies I saw when I was a kid. A life so glamorous and rich."

Sara couldn't take much more of it. It was bad enough she had to reveal this to Mitch. She owed him that much. But he hadn't even said a word. Well, not really. He was staring at her, his sympathetic blue eyes wrapping around her, as if he understood. And that's what scared the heck out of her more than anything.

He'd called her Miss Hollywood once. *Say something, Mitch.*

"You're not afraid of me?" Sara finally asked.

"Please," Mitch sputtered, his brow crinkling. "I outweigh you by what, sixty, seventy pounds?"

She drew her lips together in a wry smirk. "Who's counting? But size isn't the threat and you know it."

"What is?"

"Money. Isn't that what Lillian was after?"

"You're nothing like Lillian," he said, his face more serious than she'd ever seen it.

"From what you tell me, I'm just like her. Both of us came from poor backgrounds. She was after you for your money. I left my home for a man with money. Someone who could give me a glamorous life I thought I wanted."

If he detested her for her admission, he didn't show it. He just stared at her, his blue eyes piercing her, willing her to continue. Not because he judged her, she realized, but because he wanted to know why for her sake. Maybe his. That was more frightening.

"Dave had money. He represented everything I didn't have on the reservation. I'd look at Mandy and listen to her stories, see all the wonderful things she had and I wanted that. I truly wanted that."

"You could have had those things and lived on the reservation."

She shook her head. "Not really. I wanted everything the rez didn't give me. Couldn't give me. It wasn't that hard for me to follow Dave when he asked me to marry him."

"Did you love him?"

She wasn't shocked that he wondered, only that he actually had to ask.

"I don't think so." She laughed nervously, covering her flamed cheeks with her hands. "What does that say about me, huh? I left my family and my home for a man I didn't even love."

"You were young. People do stupid things when they're young sometimes."

"Yeah, I was young. A lot more than just young.

At the time I thought I loved him. I do believe that. Only after did I realize I just loved what he represented. A way for me to get off the rez and be the *other* part of me that was not Native American. I hated being a half-breed."

Mitch flinched slightly with her choice of words.

Her spine straightened. "Don't. You don't have to be embarrassed."

Shaking his head, he said, "I'm not. I just don't understand why you can't look at yourself as a whole person. No one in this country is full-blood anything anymore."

"I struggled with that for a long time. I didn't know which way to be. I was just so sure I had to be one or the other. No in between. No compromise. I never understood my mother's reasons for deciding to move to the reservation when she married my father. Neither one of my parents are full-blood Apache and Mom didn't even grow up on the rez. She didn't have to choose that life. I always wished she didn't because I wanted what she left behind."

"But now you're back."

Sara felt a tug at her lips and nodded. "Yeah, I guess I am. It took me a long time to figure out that the richest part of my life couldn't be measured with dollar signs and gifts. It's what I held in my heart for my home and my family."

She rose from the couch, suddenly tired, full of emotion she didn't want to face. When would that ever change? She didn't want to sit there any longer with Mitch's eyes grazing her with hunger so strong it was consuming. It wasn't just lust. Even she could see that. There was something incredible building between them. Something dangerous and frightening and exciting. Her mother had seen it, even if Sara had refused to admit to it.

She thought of the way he'd kissed her out in the workshop. How he'd held her so securely in his arms without making her feel as if she'd lost control.

She had to get out of there. To clear her head and stop thinking of Mitch as a man and how much she wanted to be in his arms again. How much she wanted to feel his tender lips against her skin and lose herself in his amazing eyes when he looked at her the way he was doing right now.

"Sara?" he called out to her from the other room.

She abruptly stopped at the base of the stairway, but didn't turn back toward the living room. *Coward!*

"I'm not afraid of you," he whispered in a deep voice just audible enough for her to hear the emotion with which he spoke.

She'd changed. She wasn't the same woman she'd been when she'd married Dave. Even she could see that. But did Mitch see that?

"Maybe you should be," she whispered to herself.

Chapter Six

The powwow was a week from Saturday. Saying that Sara was nervous was the understatement of the century. She'd rambled on for fifteen minutes to some poor soul who'd phoned and only wanted directions to the reservation. How she got the telephone number here at the ranch, Sara couldn't guess. But in her excitement, Sara had told the caller all about the powwow.

Maybe the caller was one of the other dancers who lived off the reservation. There were some who came to the powwow to compete in dance competitions and thought about the style of the dances instead of their spiritual meaning.

Sara was fully aware of the meaning of the Jingle Dance. The morning after she and Mitch had talked about her reasons for leaving Texas had been different from any other. She wasn't hiding her past anymore. She couldn't believe how wonderful it felt to be relieved of that burden.

Mitch hadn't made her feel ashamed or blamed her for anything. He just listened and took in this flawed part of her as if he'd accepted it.

She was going to dance. And although she knew her mother hoped it would be to heal her heart so she could love again, Sara knew she would dance to heal her soul, so she could forgive herself for her own past mistakes. She had changed. Her mother had seen it. More importantly, Mitch had seen it.

"Will you come to the powwow?" she asked him one morning as the day drew closer. It shouldn't have been so important to her that he be there. To watch her dance. She was doing this for herself, her own healing. But the Jingle Dance was as much for her as it would be for those who attended the powwow. And she *wanted* Mitch to see her dance.

"It means that much to you?"

Yes. She said the words in her head, wanting to say aloud what was deep in her heart. She didn't know how to define it so she let the words lie dormant, instead making a lame excuse.

"I can't watch Jonathan while I dance. I suppose my mother could, if you're too busy."

"I can keep him home if it's easier for you."

Her heart tumbled with disappointment, but she forced herself not to show it. "Jonathan's my responsibility. I won't go back on that. At least, not until someone replaces me here."

Sara thought she heard him groan or mumble. She

wasn't sure which. When he didn't offer any more than that, she went on.

"I think Jonathan might like it."

Mitch motioned to her hands as she dried the baby dish she'd just washed. "Jonathan, huh? He's just a baby. You stick that colorful dishrag on the floor and he'd be amused for an hour just trying to reach for it."

Sara chuckled softly. "Not quite. But babies love music and dancing. It's so stimulating. He'd like the singing, and the colorful costumes will catch his eye. I'd love to see his reaction to that. Wouldn't you?"

Mitch nodded, revealing a lopsided smile.

Sara squashed the surge of emotion that hit her hard. "If you have too much work—"

Rolling his eyes, he sighed and snatched the bowl she'd been drying from her hand, leaving her with the dishrag. "You women are all alike, you know that?"

Put off by his remark, Sara took a step back, staring at him. Maybe she'd been wrong to tell him about her and Dave. "How do you mean?"

He dropped the plastic baby bowl on the counter and swung around to look at her, his striking blue eyes filled with amusement. "You can't come right out and tell me you'd like *me* to see you dance? Well, I'd like to go. To see you. Not just because you can't watch Jonathan while you dance. In case you're interested, *I'd* like to see you dance. Is that okay?"

He'd turned the tables on her without her knowing it. He stood there, grinning like a fool, and she felt like even bigger one for feeling the heady zing of emotion.

"Yes, I'd like that." Sara couldn't keep from smiling. Her head was spinning and she had to remember to take a breath. "It won't be too much trouble?"

"Good Lord, Sara. No. The ranch always has something that needs doing, but nine times out of ten it can be worked around. Besides, Beau's been sticking pretty close to home these days now that Mandy is on bed rest. I can take some time."

She grabbed a dishtowel by the sink and playfully tossed it at him, holding on to her lighthearted mood. He caught it with one hand.

"You'll have a good time, you know," she said as she walked out of the kitchen to check on the baby.

Mitch watched the gentle rock of Sara's hips as she disappeared from the kitchen, then glanced at the dishtowel in his hands. It didn't much matter where he was with Sara these days. All she had to do was walk across the room and his sky lit up like fireworks set ablaze. It didn't matter if he was here or at the powwow. All it would take was being with Sara for him to have a good time.

Miss Hollywood was gone. Mitch held onto Jonathan and moved around the crowd, trying to find a good place to stand so he could watch Sara dance. She had been nervous, evident by the way she fiddled with her fingers while waiting for the other dancers to arrive.

She wanted to be early, so she and Jonathan had stayed at her mother's the night before. He'd missed her. Having a quiet house for the first time in months was something he'd taken advantage of. Or tried to.

The sun came up and he'd poured himself a bowl of corn flakes and all he could think about was coming to the reservation. Most of the Double T cowhands were at the powwow, as were Corrine and Hank. Now, as a group of dancers were finishing the Red Earth Dance, he walked through the crowd in search of some familiar faces.

He found Corrine and Hank sitting on a bench by a group of dancers and small children gathered around a young woman. Her voice drew him to her and he knew in an instant that it was Sara. She weaved a story about the sun and the stars, a girl without parents, a sky boy, and a little hummingbird. Mitch couldn't hear it all, as he was dazed by the sheer wonder of all the children sitting on the grass, their mouths agape as Sara told the Apache creation story.

Mitch's heart squeezed. Sara was truly in her element here. The storyteller teaching the children the Apache ways. It was her dream. And he understood a lot about dreams, because he had his own.

As he moved to the back of the crowd, Sara lifted her head and when her dark mystical eyes met his, she smiled. Never once did she waver from her story. But that one smile dragged him in. Although he was standing in the back of the crowd, it was as if he was sitting beside her. Her voice rose and fell to almost a whisper, passionate and exciting.

Guilt stabbed at him. He wanted Sara to stay at the Double T. But this was where she really belonged.

Jonathan started to fuss and Mitch jiggled him up and down just a little, to keep him from letting out a howl that would surely bring Sara to his side and put an abrupt end to the story.

An announcement came over the intercom that dancers would begin the Jingle Dance. Sara stood up and a group of children rushed to her, hugging her legs before their parents peeled them off so she could make her way to the dancing area.

Miss Hollywood was definitely gone, Mitch thought as Sara stood in the dance area with the other women who would perform the Jingle Dance. She'd tried so hard to blend in. She hadn't succeeded, to his way of thinking. Sara was off-the-scale beautiful in every way he could name, whether she was wearing the silk suit and fancy gold sandals she'd picked up in L.A. or this colorful red and blue jingle dress. She was simultaneously sophisticated and innocent, reflective of both the worlds she'd lived in.

The music started with the drumbeat that was the backbone of most Native American dances. Sara's movement among the other dancers was controlled. With the heavy beat of the drum, their moccasined feet came down on the hard earth and the hundreds of little metal fringes on the dresses fell against each other, making a sound almost like rain hitting a tin roof. The dance went on. Mitch wasn't sure if Sara was even aware of the people around her in the crowd. She seemed lost, somewhere on her own.

But he was with her, where she was. She was beautiful. He wondered if he'd ever told her that, just how beautiful she really was. He lifted Jonathan up higher on his shoulder and patted his son's back. He would tell her tonight, Mitch decided. Suddenly the idea of spending the day at the powwow seemed much too long. Now all he could think about was taking Sara home so he could have her all to himself.

They stayed the whole day, Hank reconnecting with old friends and family members, Sara introducing both

Mitch and Jonathan to her relatives. The magic of the day had begun with Mitch opening his eyes to see just how special Sara was.

But he'd never told her that. Not really. And he wasn't exactly sure how he felt about it. Only that he really didn't want her to leave.

With Jonathan sleeping against his shoulder and Sara saying the last of her good-byes, they left the powwow. Hank, Corrine, and the rest of the cowpokes from the Double T headed out just behind them. Jonathan hadn't even stirred when Mitch put him in the car seat and strapped him in between Sara and himself. With any luck, his son would sleep through a diaper change and then go down nice and easy.

"You're beautiful," Mitch said. They had been back from the powwow for all of twenty minutes. Mitch seemed like he was in an awful hurry to get Jonathan to bed. Sara would have preferred to have given him a bottle so that he would sleep through the night. But she had to admit she too was anxious to get Jonathan to bed so she could spend a little time alone with Mitch.

They'd met so many people at the powwow, so many faces she hadn't seen in years. She hadn't had much time to talk to Mitch. She'd danced the Jingle Dance and she knew that he was watching her. She had caught a glimpse of him just once as she brought the colorful fan to her face at the end of the dance. She'd never forget those eyes. The way he looked at her, the honey warmth of his dark blue eyes. It was the way he was looking at her now.

"You're really outdoing yourself tonight, cowboy."

His face was dark, shadowy, and sexy as she'd ever seen it. "You must want something from me."

His lips tilted to a wry grin, a slow, sexy spread, making her knees grow weak. "I do." Hooking his arm around her waist, he dragged her close. Somewhere deep down, Sara told herself she shouldn't let it happen. She shouldn't want Mitch to kiss her, but she did. And she knew that was exactly what he was intending.

He didn't push the headband from her forehead as she thought he'd do. He just held her, studied her with his eyes, drinking her in. He brushed his thumb across her brow and slowly down her cheek, making her head spin and her breath catch in the spot in her throat where her pulse pounded.

"Talk to me."

It wasn't at all what she'd expected. Mitch had a way of giving her the unexpected. She chuckled.

"What is it you want me to say?"

"Anything. Tell me one of your stories."

Her brow furrowed. "You want me to tell you a story?"

"Yeah, how about the one you told today to the kids? Wait, no, tell the one about the eagle who soared to the sky. The one you were telling Jonathan when he couldn't take his eyes off you."

Cocking her head to one side, she said, "Why do you want to hear that story again?"

She inched herself away from him, but he only reeled her back, close to him.

"Because I like hearing your voice. I like listening to you talk in that soft whisper. It's almost like a song. It's . . . sexy." He brushed his lips against her cheek. "Talk to me, Sara."

She lifted her arms and wrapped them around his shoulders. Everything about Mitch was strong, from the well-defined muscles of his arms as he held her to the conviction in his soul. He made her feel safe, and Sara hadn't felt that in a long time. She hadn't felt the embrace of a man without feeling trapped or too intimidated to enjoy the feeling. This she liked. She couldn't know for sure, but if she chose to step back out of his arms now, he'd let her go. And because of that, she didn't feel threatened.

"This could complicate things," she said, staring up into his eyes.

"It's already complicated."

"I don't want to . . ."

"What? Tell me."

She hesitated a moment, feeling the muscles of his arms bunch with frustration.

"Don't back away from me now, Sara. This is too important."

"I don't want to feel trapped again."

He nodded, locking his gaze on her. "You can walk away any time. I'm not holding you in chains. I never would."

"Mitch," she whispered above the musical jingle of her dress as she moved closer.

She lifted on her toes and brushed a kiss across his lips ever so slightly, just a breath of a whisper. He turned his head to capture her lips but she moved away.

She was testing him. She couldn't be sure why and he didn't seem to mind. She didn't want to talk. She wanted to melt there in Mitch's arms and let the lure of his kisses drag her reserve away.

And then he did. Mitch slowly lowered his head until his mouth was inches from hers.

"I like the way you say my name."

"Want me to say it again?"

He nodded.

She whispered his name in his ear.

"I'll take that as an invitation if you don't mind."

"Please do," she whispered just as his mouth crushed over hers.

It was powerful; more so than Sara had imagined possible. How could two hearts collide with the force of bursting stars? But there they were, his heart merging with hers. She knew the difference between a kiss for wanting something and a kiss born of emotion.

A knock on the door dragged her back into consciousness. She didn't want to come back down to earth and break free of this union. She wanted to hold on to Mitch.

"The door," she said, pulling from his kiss.

"I didn't hear it," he said, holding fast to her, keeping her from bolting, but allowing her to do so if she decided. She liked that about him. He *didn't* control her. It amazed her how much trust she put in that after what she'd gone through with Dave.

The next knock on the door was more pronounced.

"Go away, Beau. I'm not here!" Mitch yelled. She couldn't help but giggle as he dragged her back into his arms and began kissing her again.

"It's not Beau."

Mitch stiffened in her arms. It was enough to make all the magic of their kiss fade and her heart plummet.

"Mitch?" the female voice called again.

"Who is it, Mitch?" Sara asked, somehow knowing that it would have been better not to ask.

"Lillian."

Chapter Seven

Of all times, why did Lillian have to show up now?

"I'm sorry, Sara."

The knock on the door was unrelenting now. Lillian hated to wait.

"You'd better answer the door then."

With a heavy sigh, Mitch dropped his arms from Sara's waist. It was as if he'd let go of a piece of himself.

Running his hand over his head, he stalked to the door and yanked it open.

Lillian stood there in designer shoes that probably cost more than a week's grocery bill for the entire ranch. Her hair was slicked back and secured at the nape of her neck with a bright red silk scarf.

"Aren't you going to invite me in?"

"What do you want, Lillian?"

She glanced past him into the kitchen and stared at Sara, who was still standing where he'd kissed her. She was still there. Mitch was glad of that, although he knew it shouldn't have made a difference.

"I came to see my son."

As if it were timed just that way, Jonathan began crying from his crib. Sara quickly flew from the room to attend to him.

"Your son? So now he's your son? What about two months ago when you dropped him off in the arms of strangers like an old suitcase? Was he your son then, too?"

Her smile was flat.

"Of course, silly."

He heard Jonathan's cry from upstairs. And within seconds the sound grew louder. Fear clutched his gut. Had she brought the baby down? Hadn't he told Sara that Lillian was capable of anything? Lillian never did anything unless it benefited her.

"Pocahontas seems like . . . an interesting girl, Mitch."

She pushed her way past him into the room. His house suddenly felt so invaded, so exposed.

"Her name is Sara, and you leave her out of this."

"If she is caring for my child, she's already in it. Or is she here in some other capacity?"

"That's none of your business."

"I have rights—"

"You threw away all rights when you tossed Jonathan on my doorstep without a word. What kind of mother does that to a kid? You didn't even leave a note or word of when you'd be back. If ever!"

"Did you think that sort of treatment was only reserved for fathers?"

Her words stung as if she'd slapped his face. Mitch had confided in Lillian about his father's abuse. Why wouldn't he? He thought he was marrying a woman with whom he could trust his deepest fears. What started out as the hope of a lifetime together had lasted merely two weeks before the deception began.

"I want you to leave. Now."

"Not until I see my son."

Mitch let the door slam shut, shoving his clenched hands deep into the pockets of his jeans. He walked in front of Lillian to keep her from wandering any farther into the house.

Jonathan's crying was loud from in the next room.

"Mitch?" Sara said softly from behind. But he ignored her call.

"What makes you think I'm going to trust him with you after what you did? Haven't you hurt him enough?"

"You have no choice."

"Maybe not before he was born, but I do now. And right now I don't want you anywhere near my son," he boomed.

Jonathan's screaming, sharp and piercing, cut through Mitch like a knife. But it was his fault.

It was rare for Mitch to lose his temper. It reminded him too much of his old man and how scared he'd been when his parents fought. As a child, Mitch would run and hide under the bed, or pull all his toys out of the closet and sit in the dark and cry. This time, his voice had brought on the tears. Deep regret coursed through him with the thought of what he'd done, and he wished he could snatch his anger back. *Stay in control.*

"I just want to see my baby. That's all." In an instant, Lillian's face had changed, no doubt because now she had an audience. She had a look of longing in her eyes when she glanced over at Jonathan in Sara's arms. Mitch closed his eyes in defeat.

"Please?"

He didn't want to, but he glanced back at Sara then. Her dark brown eyes were pleading with him, her bottom lip trembling slightly. She didn't want to hand his son over to Lillian.

His son.

Mitch's shoulders sagged. No matter how much he wanted to claim Jonathan for himself, to protect him from the mother who most surely would only hurt him, Jonathan was Lillian's son too.

Mitch didn't want to think of Jonathan that way. He'd grown up with the fighting, his father always walking out the door.

Then the waiting started. Mitch would come home from school and race to the mailbox, hoping to find a letter or a card. With every car that pulled into his driveway, Mitch was sure his father was coming home to him. But he never did.

There was so much disappointment when his dad broke his promises. It wasn't until Mitch was a teenager that he realized the only person he could count on was himself.

He didn't want that for Jonathan. And he didn't want Jonathan to carry a legacy of anger between his parents throughout his whole life either.

He met Sara's pleading gaze and nodded once, feeling his gut clench so tight that he could hardly breathe as Sara placed Jonathan in Lillian's arms.

Lillian held Jonathan tight and looked down at him, kissing his forehead as a mother would after not seeing her child for a while. Mitch looked away.

"I missed you so much, darling," Lillian said in a low crooning voice.

Fear leveled him. Mitch knew this was what he had feared the most, why he hadn't wanted to open his heart to his son in the first place. He knew Lillian too well. This was her intention all along.

"You can't have him back."

He reached out his arms, ready to snatch his child from Lillian. Anything to have his son back again without fear.

But Lillian backed up a step, out of his reach.

His pulse thrummed wildly and he felt the primal need to protect his child.

"He's my son, too, Mitch. You can't shut me out of his life."

"What do you really want?"

Lillian might have missed Sara's soft gasp, but to Mitch it echoed around him in a desperate plea.

He didn't want to look at Sara, didn't want to see those dark eyes asking him to do what he didn't want to do.

Instead, he held his gaze hard and forceful on Lillian. Jonathan began to scream again and it was all Mitch could do to keep from lunging forward and yanking him away.

"Hand over my son."

"Or you'll do what?" Lillian arched a thinly lined brow in challenge. He'd once thought that was an attractive gesture; now he knew the wickedness behind it.

"We both know you don't want him, Lillian. Otherwise, you wouldn't have left him here in the first place."

"You two need some time alone," Sara said quietly behind him.

"No, don't go, Sara," Mitch said at the same time Lillian replied, "I think that's best."

Say, something, he silently pleaded to Sara. *If you care at all for this child, for me, then say something*. He hated the helplessness he felt. He didn't want to be there. It was like being eight years old again and hiding in the closet.

But Sara remained silent by the kitchen doorway, just staring at Jonathan while he screamed and screamed, as if she were about to scream herself. Abruptly, she darted to the refrigerator and seized a bottle already filled with formula.

"He hasn't had his bottle yet," Sara said nervously. "He's hungry, that's all."

She unscrewed the cap off the bottle and placed it in the microwave. As the microwave hummed, Mitch took a long step forward and lifted his son from his mother's arms. Relief washed over him, but an underlying uneasiness remained.

He hated the look on Sara's face when he handed Jonathan to her. She just stared at him, unshed tears clinging to her dark eyes, pleading with him. Then she looked at Lillian. Jonathan started crying again and suddenly all her attention was focused on the baby.

Mitch had thought Sara was going to feed the bottle to Jonathan. But from the bewildered look in her eye when he handed the baby to her, it was clear she'd prepared the bottle so that Lillian could feed him.

"Please take Jonathan upstairs to bed," Mitch said quietly.

She nodded. "Okay," she said in a voice much too shaky for his liking.

He noticed the slight unsteadiness of her step as she left, and he wished she didn't have to be part of this whole scene.

"Okay, out with it. What do you really want, Lillian?" he asked when they were finally alone.

Her chuckle was low and quick. "You offend me."

"You do a pretty good job of that yourself by playing games. At least, that's the way I remember it."

"Is this any way to treat your long-lost wife?"

"Ex-wife. It was a mistake that lasted two weeks. That's why it was annulled."

"That was my mistake. See, if I'd only known that your rich grandfather really *did* have a pile of money, I'd have hired myself a good divorce lawyer instead of letting you talk me into that annulment."

Mitch shook his head. "You know as well as I do that our marriage was a mistake. It never would have worked."

Lillian chuckled wryly. "That much is true. If I had to live my whole life holed up here in some dusty Texas town I'd have gone mad."

"Then why are you here now?"

"I told you. I wanted to see my son."

Mitch let out a slow sigh and quickly glanced at the kitchen door. "Well, now you have," he said quietly.

"And I think Jonathan deserves to get some of that money your grandfather willed you."

"What will? I told you the day I came home and found someone else on my side of the bed that my grandpa's lawyer never drew up a will. And except for the few investments he had, which no doubt my dad has already lost in Atlantic City, my grandfather lived his last days on social security."

"No wonder your father was able to hurt you so badly. You're far too gullible, Mitch."

"And I want you to leave. Now," he said, through clenched teeth.

"Not until my son gets everything that's coming to him."

"Everything I have is his."

Her lips twisted into a satisfied grin. "That's what I'm counting on."

"That doesn't include you."

She glared hard at him, but he didn't back down or make apologies for his behavior. Her lips pursed wryly. "Still upset that I forgot to tell you about him, are you?"

"You didn't forget anything. With you, everything is a calculated move. What I can't figure out is the timing. Why did you wait until he was a few weeks old to tell me about him?"

"You're the one who left Baltimore."

He shook his head in disbelief. "You knew how to find me. You could have called. I would have been there for you."

She glanced up at him, and for a split second, he saw the young girl he knew as a child. "Would you have? Even after the way things ended for us?"

In truth, Mitch wasn't sure. It was all a bit of a blur, like when he'd come home from the nursing home after visiting his grandfather to find his wife with another man. Before that, he'd seen what he needed to see in Lillian. Only then did he see the true woman he'd married. He was glad when she'd so readily agreed to an annulment.

Lillian settled herself in a chair at the kitchen table and fingered the delicate tablecloth Sara had placed on it. "Your lady friend has nice taste."

"I told you to leave Sara out of this."

With a roll of her eyes, she began rifling through her purse and after a moment, pulled out a compact and a tube of lipstick. She reapplied another layer of red over her already colored lips while she spoke.

"I'm surprised you even want to be saddled with a kid. All those plans of yours to have your own ranch and train horses doesn't leave much time for being a daddy. But you'd talked about how much having a family one day meant to you. It was too late to have—"

The glare he shot stopped her from finishing.

Lillian sighed and went on, ignoring him. "I almost didn't have him, you know, but I did. I must have gotten pregnant on our wedding night and I didn't even know until after you'd already left for Texas. You were so angry, I figured it would only make things worse. I was all ready to give him up for adoption, I figured you'd really hate me then."

"Does that matter to you?"

"We were friends once upon a time. But then I wasn't sure you'd even want Jonathan."

"He's my son. Besides, what choice did you leave me? You blew out the door like a tornado the first chance you got."

"You could have shipped him back to Baltimore."

"Oh, now that's very maternal of you."

She gave him a hard look sugarcoated with sweetness. "I never said I was. But he is my son."

"If seeing him is what you want, I'll have my lawyer draw up some visitation agreement and you can visit."

She laughed. A chill raced through his veins and up his spine. The woman he remembered leaving in Baltimore was back. She had a plan, an agenda and Mitch wanted no part of it.

"Not visitation. I want him back."

Mitch felt as if the wind had been knocked out of him. "You're not leaving this ranch with Jonathan."

"I'm sorry to hear you talk like that, Mitch. I was hoping we could come to an agreement on our own."

"I think we're both too emotional about Jonathan to talk rationally to each other."

"Perhaps. But lawyers can make things so messy and they are so expensive. If you stop and think clearly about what's best for Jonathan, I'm sure we'll be able to work something out."

He shook his head and walked to the door. "I don't happen to agree with you on that one. More importantly, I don't trust you."

With practiced grace, she stretched her legs out from beneath the table and stood. "I'm sorry to hear you say that. But not half as sorry as you'll be when I'm through with you."

"What's that supposed to mean?"

"You of all people should know that when I want something I don't stop until I get it. It's something we both shared, something you once said was what attracted you to me."

His fists clenched at his side, he leveled her with a hard gaze as she spun on her designer heels through the door without another word. Looking back, Lillian smiled and then slammed the door in her wake.

Mitch hadn't realized how fast and hard his heart was pumping until he was alone in the silence.

Good God, she wanted to take his son away. His son. But as Lillian had pointed out, Jonathan was her son too.

His hands were trembling as he poured a glass of water and quickly gulped it down. He had to see Jonathan. Watching Lillian and hearing her threats had brought back way too many memories he didn't want to face, shaking him to the core.

The light in the room had gone dim with the fading day. Jonathan had fallen asleep after only half a bottle, well before the yelling had stopped. Sara had sat quietly rocking him until she heard the kitchen door slam. She placed him in the crib and peered out the window. As Lillian's car sped away, Sara expelled a heavy sigh of relief that it was over. She couldn't face hearing any more bickering over Jonathan. He was just a baby, an innocent.

But mostly, Sara couldn't stay because no matter how much she knew Mitch was angry and how frightened she was by Lillian's appearance, she didn't share his feelings.

She'd seen the longing in Lillian's eyes when she glanced at Jonathan. It must have been hard for her to see him after such a long time, seen how much he'd changed and how he'd bonded with a total stranger. After two months, it was as if he didn't even know his mother was holding him.

But Lillian was Jonathan's mother, not her. She'd known that all along, obviously. But until now, Lillian had been just a name. She wasn't a living, breathing person who could make decisions and make mistakes, just like she had. She wasn't a beautiful woman that Mitch had loved and had a child with. Even though in her mind Sara knew she existed, Lillian hadn't been real. Until now.

She sank down into the rocking chair by Jonathan's crib and pushed back with a sigh. Jonathan was sound asleep and would probably remain that way until the morning. He was such a good baby that way.

And Mitch, although he'd balked at the idea of being a father, had stepped into the role with ease. Now it was as if Jonathan had always been a part of his life. He had to be scared to death of losing him.

Leaning forward in the rocker, Sara stared at the precious baby she'd come to love so dearly. The resemblance to Mitch was undeniable. But there had to be signs of his mother there, too. She searched the baby's face and her memory for traces of Lillian in Jonathan's features and came up blank. Oh, she knew Lillian was there. And as Jonathan grew and changed, more of his mother would emerge. But for right now, this little cowboy was the spitting image of his daddy.

That made the illusion easier. An illusion that had been shattered as Mitch had his arms wound securely around her.

Sara could almost still feel the hard, corded muscles

of Mitch's shoulders jump underneath her touch when she'd reached up and kissed him earlier. Unconsciously, she drew in a breath and the memory of his aftershave filled her. She'd opened up her heart and let Mitch Broader in, despite her best intentions.

Her goal had been so clear. She was going home. But now her heart was crying out for something different yet again. How could that be? She couldn't possibly be doomed to continue making the same mistake over and over again.

It was only a matter of weeks before she'd start visiting the schools on the rez. As soon as word got out, she knew she'd probably get offers from schools in the surrounding area to tell the stories that were being lost to this new generation of Apache children. She still wanted all that. But she wanted Mitch, too. Now that Lillian was here in Texas, what would that mean for all of them? Where did she fit in?

The creak in the top stair signaled that Mitch was just outside her bedroom door. She'd heard the kitchen door slam and the car roar down the driveway. Sara had to admit she'd let out a sigh of relief that Jonathan was still sleeping in his crib. She had no right to that feeling.

Mitch appeared at the doorway. His face no longer held that ferocious look of a lion protecting his cub. The rough lines of his face and his drawn expression showed both how weary and relieved he was.

He didn't say a word. He just walked over to the crib and laid a gentle hand on Jonathan's belly as he slept. He stood there for a long moment in silence, just watching. Finally, he turned and glanced at Sara.

"You should turn in," he whispered. "It's been a long day and you look exhausted."

"So do you."

He simply nodded, then walked out of the room. The magic of the day was gone.

Chapter Eight

It had been a restless night for both of them. Sara didn't have to notice the slight bend in his shoulders, or the heaviness of his eyes to know Mitch had thought long hours into the night about Lillian's visit.

She had, too. Much as she knew it was none of her business, she couldn't help but wonder how this visit from Lillian would change both her life and Mitch's.

He'd never gotten to tell her what he'd wanted to say yesterday. They'd been interrupted by the doorbell. But these past few days had felt almost magical in a way Sara hadn't thought ever possible again. She was sure Mitch was going to ask her to stay. He'd kept himself back from asking. He was fiercely independent that way. She understood too well what had driven him there. She experienced a similar kind of betrayal and knew how much he valued his hard-won self-esteem.

The cockiness of a man who knew where he was going and what he was doing didn't mask the pained little boy who'd been left to handle emotional bruises. It was there. And she . . . yes, she loved him both for it and because of what he'd managed to do in spite of it. Mitchell Broader was a good man. He had his reasons for not giving Lillian a second chance.

It was all the more reason they had to talk. But before she could broach the subject after breakfast, Mitch had quickly disappeared to work with Beau.

She'd wait for him, Sara decided. He was able to ignore his problems out on the range, and maybe that would give him time to clear his head, but he had to come home eventually. His reason for coming home was right here in her arms.

She glanced down at Jonathan, who had just successfully drained the last of his bottle. He was such a beautiful baby. In the last month, since she knew her feelings for Mitch were growing by leaps and bounds, she'd allowed herself to imagine them as a family. What would it be like to give this precious child she'd fallen so in love with a sister or brother? What kind of hair would a child they created have? Would their child have Mitch's blue eyes or take more after her and inherit her striking Apache features?

It didn't matter any more. She wasn't Jonathan's mother. And no matter how much she would love to think otherwise, Jonathan was the thread that had bound her and Mitch together. Without it, they would fall apart.

An ache settled, dull but strong, in the center of her chest.

"You knew this could happen, Sara," she whispered as she placed the baby in his crib. "All the more reason why you don't belong here."

Mitch wouldn't be happy about what Sara was going to tell him, but he had to know her true feelings. If she didn't tell him, then they'd have nothing. No chance for any kind of future.

As she closed the door to the nursery, she wondered if even that had been an illusion all along.

Sara visited with Mandy only briefly. Now that she was on bed rest as she neared the end of her pregnancy, there wasn't a whole lot she could do besides sleep and read. Sara had sat at the foot of Mandy's new four-poster bed and chatted for a while, wanting so much to tell Mandy about Lillian's visit, but feeling too disjointed to put her jumbled thoughts into words.

Although Mandy had confessed to hearing Lillian's car spin out of the driveway the night before, after everyone had come home from the powwow, she hadn't pressed the issue. Sara was glad for that.

And she was glad later when Corrine insisted she leave Jonathan with her while Sara brought the cowboys some lunch out in the fields. She was doing her a huge favor, Corrine had said. Besides, Alice was coming over and the two of them needed to do some spoiling.

Sara had loaded Corrine's pickup truck with a picnic basket full of sandwiches and drinks. As she made her way up the rutted dirt road toward the pasture where they'd been baling hay all morning, her stomach clenched. She was glad when she found Mitch and Beau alone and learned that the other hands had headed back to the ranch for lunch.

Mitch's blue eyes registered panic when she climbed out of the truck.

"What's wrong?"

Beau tipped his hat to her. "Good afternoon, Sara. What brings you out here?"

"Where's Jonathan?"

"Back at the house with Corrine. He's fine and quite happy being the center of attention."

Mitch's face instantly registered relief. "I thought . . ."

He shook his head and pulled off his gloves as he walked over to her. The lines she'd seen etched in the corner of his eyes had smoothed some, despite being under the hot sun. Now he smiled one of those brilliant smiles that had the power to melt her.

Despite the cowboy hat protected his fair-skinned face from the sun, Sara immediately noticed that Mitch's upper arms were starting to burn.

"I'm glad you stopped by then," he said, his eyes grazing her with a hunger she'd felt herself just the evening before.

She actually felt her heart flutter. Vaguely aware that Beau was standing nearby, she said, "There's lunch in the picnic basket. And some sunscreen to keep you both from looking like a snake shedding his skin."

"Good, because I'm starving and he's sunburned," Beau said.

She waited until she saw Beau settled in the front

seat of the pickup, sifting through the food Corrine had prepared.

"You need to get some sunscreen on you or you're going to be hurting later," she said quickly.

"I've missed you," he responded.

He pulled her into his arms, ignoring her unspoken warning. She settled against him; they fit like a glove. She liked the feel of this glove. She wondered how long it would last.

"You left early this morning."

He kissed her gently on the lips and said, "I know. I have a lot of work ahead of me. Beau and I want to have some time to work with the horses tonight. Some of them are ready to show."

"What about Jonathan?"

"You can bring him on out to the corral to watch his old man." His grin was bright. "It won't be long before he'll be testing the saddle himself. Might as well give him his first ride."

Sara chuckled. "You don't think he's too young?"

"Heck, no. Lots of Texas cowboys start riding from the cradle. Will you bring him out and come for a ride with us?"

She didn't answer right away. He was stalling. And right at that moment, Sara realized it was the wrong time for her to talk to him about what was on her mind.

When she hesitated, Mitch tipped her chin up with the tip of his fingers. "In case you're wondering, I'm asking you on a date."

She blinked, trying hard not to do something so utterly ridiculous as sigh. "And using your son as a ruse to get me to go riding?"

"Oh, Jonathan will be riding. But I'm going to make sure I get a few rides in with you, too. Trust me?"

"Yes," she said much too quickly for her liking.

They still needed to talk. But maybe after they spent some time together tonight, it would be the perfect time for them to do it. By then, maybe she'd have her head on straight enough to know exactly how she felt.

Sara had raced through the day like a giddy schoolgirl, and yet, part of her knew she should be keeping herself much in check. He'd called it a date. It wasn't a date. Not really. She wouldn't make it a date. Not yet, anyway.

She knew all too well that her feelings for Mitch were growing. With Lillian's sudden appearance yesterday, she'd make sure that she clamped down any notion to encourage him until she knew exactly how they both felt. It would only complicated matters more if they rushed into another relationship with unfinished business left behind.

But Mitch's kiss. Sara couldn't stop thinking about it. It had been sweet and gentle and full of excitement. Something deep inside her burst free like a volcanic eruption. She remembered the feel of his arms as they slipped protectively around her waist and pulled her close to him. It had been like coming home. Like a rebirth of something she'd lost long ago and didn't know how to find again.

She shook her head as she folded yet more baby clothes to hand over to Mandy. Jonathan was growing by leaps and bounds. Her heart squeezed with an emotion she knew she shouldn't name. She loved the baby, just like . . .

No, it was natural for her to fall in love with the baby. She was his caregiver and it was only right that she gave him all her attention and her heart as well. He'd been denied a mother, but he deserved a mother's love. Even if she would only be staying for a little while. None of that meant that she was in love with his father.

Mitch. She wondered just how long she could stay in Mitchell Broader's home before she couldn't ignore the truth any longer. She was desperately falling in love with him, too.

Mitch showered and changed before dinner. Normally, if he were going to work the horses, he'd just hold off until the day was done and he could spend some time with his son. And Sara. Yes, he was giving himself a little more care than usual because he hoped that Sara would indulge him. What they'd started last night as he held her was only a beginning.

Lord, what was he going to do with her? he mused as he pulled on his boots. She had her heart set on going to the reservation. After seeing her during the powwow ceremony, talking to all the native children and keeping them spellbound, he had to wonder where he and Jonathan fit into the equation.

He'd seen Jonathan in her arms countless times, listening to her tell her stories—not that Jonathan understood a word of it, Mitch thought, chuckling quietly to himself. He just liked the sound of her voice and the gentleness of her.

Yeah, Mitch liked that, too. He loved the way her eyes flashed bright with excitement. And he loved that drugged gaze she gave him when he pressed his lips against hers, and the way she melted into his embrace like warm honey spreading over him. With all he was, he hadn't wanted to let go of her last night. Not ever.

But then Lillian showed up. It had been a major jolt to his peace of mind. He knew he was being hard. Lillian was Jonathan's mother and he had to give her some ounce of respect for that.

Because Mitch had grown up around all his parents' mudslinging, he knew that that kind of bitterness would only hurt his son. He wouldn't do that to Jonathan. When he'd looked into Sara's pleading eyes last night, he knew that's what she was telling him.

Okay, so if Lillian wanted to drop by now and then, he'd let her. He knew her too well to think that she'd tire of it soon enough. He only hoped that he'd be able to keep his son from being brokenhearted over it.

Well, enough worrying about Lillian, Mitch thought as he strode downstairs. He had an appointment with Cody Gentry, Beau's brother, about buying some of the horses he'd worked. The deal with Hank was that the Double T got first dibs on any of the horses Mitch trained. Beau kept a few green horses for the rodeo school. After that, it was Mitch's business to sell them to whomever he pleased and pocket the money.

It was a sweet deal for him as any money from the sale of horses would go right back into the bank towards his own spread. Mitch was fervently determined to meet his goal. By his estimation, he'd have what he needed in two, maybe three years, provided he could sell enough horses.

Mitch was both surprised and elated when Beau mentioned the Silverado Cattle Company, his father's spread, was looking to buy a few horses of their own.

Beau had dropped Mitch's name to his brother, figuring his old man would shoot the idea down pronto, which, of course, Mike Gentry had. But then Cody had up and called Mitch on his own, saying he'd heard of his reputation and wanted to see for himself what Mitch had to offer. The fact that he trained on Double T soil didn't bother Cody like it bothered Mike Gentry.

To Mitch, it was a great opportunity to further his business. Not only did the Silverado Cattle Company have the deep pockets to spend top dollar, they had connections far beyond Steerage Rock. That was something Mitch was counting on. Word of mouth in this business meant much more than the bottom line. He'd give Cody a fair price and a fine horse.

Smiling, Mitch joined his family at the dinner table.

"It's still early, but I have to get this baby to bed pretty soon or he'll be over-tired and I'll have to rock him to sleep," Sara said.

She had Jonathan in the front pack. The little bonnet on his head, protecting his head from the sun and any dust the wind kicked up, kept tipping off and falling to the dirt each and every time Mitch road by on Midnight. Sara finally gave up and stuffed the bonnet in her pocket, keeping her hand protectively on the baby's delicate head.

"My boy has you whipped," Mitch called out from his mount. "I'd choose you rocking me over settling in bed alone."

Her cheeks flamed and she was glad Cody and Beau were talking to each other far enough away that they hadn't heard.

"Behave yourself in front of your son, Mr. Broader."

Mitch's lips tilted into a wickedly sexy grin that made her blood run like hot rain from her toes to her hairline.

"Care to take a ride before you turn in?" His cobalt blue eyes twinkled with specks of crimson from the setting sun. He cast her a smile so sexy that her heart raced wildly and her pulse hammered in her ear.

"I think I'll pass tonight."

Beau had come up behind her with Cody.

"Sure I can't talk you out of selling Midnight?" Cody asked Mitch. Cody Gentry was as tall as his brother and had the same strong, muscular build. Though there were distinct differences in the two, it was hard not to see they were brothers. Sara was sure there were more than a few women in Steerage Rock and beyond who had their eye on Cody Gentry.

"Nah, I've got someone in mind for her," Mitch said.

"Whatever his price is, I'll double it. She sure is a beautiful animal," Cody said, leaning his arm on the rail to peer at Midnight.

"Sorry," Mitch said as he got off his mount. "This one is Sara's."

"Mine?" Sara gasped.

"Sure. She's a gift for you."

"But . . ."

Cody chuckled. "Guess I'm talking to the wrong person. Darlin', any time you want to do business on this pretty thing, you just let me know."

"Why don't you let me take the baby in to see Mandy?" Beau was saying as Sara tried to find her voice. "She's got those nesting instincts. At least that's what Corrine calls it. I have to admit, I can't wait for the chance to have one of these in my arms. If I had my way, Mandy would be having our baby tonight," he said, taking Jonathan from Sara.

"We'll be by in a while to bring him home."

Mitch was staring at her, Sara realized. What was he thinking giving her this horse? Not to mention the money he'd passed up not selling it to the Silverado Cattle Company.

When they were alone, she waited next to the corral gate for Mitch to ride the horse by so she could talk with him without anyone overhearing. She stuffed her hands in her pocket in anticipation.

"Mitch," she said, looking up at his bright smile. He was pleased with himself. She could tell he wanted her to have Midnight. "I can't accept this horse."

His spirits didn't waver. "Why not? Don't you like her?"

"She's beautiful."

"Not half as beautiful as you, Sara."

Heat crept up her neck and burned her cheeks. He had to stop doing that. "Mitch, I don't have any place to keep a horse."

"Keep her here. That way you have an excuse to come back and visit," he said, sliding down from his mount. He wasn't looking at her now. But Sara could tell he was testing her.

"I'm going back to the reservation."

"I know that." He looked at her then and what she saw was emotion, not anger. His voice was quiet, blending in with the sounds of the coming night. She'd told him straight out and he didn't charge back at her to intimidate her. It was one of the things she loved about him.

She sighed.

"Just because you're leaving some day doesn't mean you can't come back and visit."

She stared at him for a moment, emotion waging war inside her. Could she come back? It was a dangerous thought. She was already too close to both Mitch and Jonathan. Flitting in and out of their lives would only confuse them.

"It wouldn't be the same."

"No, it wouldn't," he said. "But you know what I want. There's no need for me to say more than that. I just wanted to give you Midnight as a present. She's like you. She's incredibly gentle, and her eyes flash like firecrackers when she's excited. And when she neighs it's like she's singing. Just like you."

Her bottom lip trembled. It was an incredibly beautiful thing to say. And the fact that Mitch gifted her with Midnight for that reason made it impossible for her to resist.

"Come ride with me. You'll see she's meant for you."

Her heart couldn't tell her different.

Mitch reached out to take her hand.

"Together?"

"Sure. That way I have a valid excuse to hold you close."

She climbed onto the front of Midnight's saddle. Mitch slipped on the back. As he wrapped his arms around her to take the reins, she was engulfed by his warmth and spirit and she suddenly had the urge to run far away. She wasn't ready for this. Wasn't ready to open up her heart for more heartache. She'd made that mistake once before, hadn't she?

"You want to take control? You can take her anywhere you please."

What pleased her was sitting there snuggled up against Mitch. She turned her head back and he nuzzled his whiskered cheek against hers, giving her a quick kiss before placing the reins in her hands.

He let her lead. Mitch was good that way. He let her know what he wanted for sure. But the decision was always hers. She was always free to walk away.

And she hadn't. She'd stayed here at the Double T when she could have had someone at the ranch to care for Jonathan within a week of her arrival.

Why hadn't she? It didn't make sense. She hadn't tried hard enough to find a replacement for herself because deep down, this is where she wanted to be. How had her plans to go back to the reservation been derailed so quickly?

Instead of giving in to self-deprecation, she reveled in the feel of Mitch's corded muscles as he helped her maneuver Midnight around the corral.

She was so entranced in the quiet moment, the feeling of just being with Mitch, listening to the clip-clop of Midnight's hooves as she danced around the corral, that she didn't notice Lillian's approach. And apparently, neither had Mitch.

"Just what do you think you're doing?" Lillian boomed.

Sara snapped her gaze to the edge of the corral and felt her heart sink to the dirt. There was absolutely nothing wrong with her being here like this with Mitch. Mitch and Lillian were no longer married. But suddenly Sara felt as if she were caught red-handed stealing cookies from the cookie jar.

Lillian dropped to the ground and picked up Jonathan's bonnet, which must have fallen from her pocket when she entered the corral. "And just who is taking care of my son?"

Chapter Nine

"Jonathan's fine, Lillian."

"Where is he?"

"You abandoned him, why should you care?"

She reached into her purse and pulled out an envelope. "This piece of paper says otherwise."

Mitch rode Midnight over to where Lillian stood and dismounted. Sara quickly followed.

"What are you up to now, Lillian?"

"Read for yourself."

Sara watched as Mitch's face turned to horror. "Why you—" He stopped himself short. Mitch wasn't a man to curse like she'd heard many a man in her life. She'd yet to hear him use a foul word in front of her in all the time they'd spent together.

"What is it, Mitch?" she asked, afraid of the answer.

"A summons to appear in court for custody of Jonathan." His voice was tight and controlled, like he always was, but Sara wasn't sure he felt anything that resembled control. "And an order to bring him back to Baltimore within forty-eight hours."

"If you don't want this to turn into kidnapping charges, I suggest you comply."

"Kidnapping?" Sara gasped. "You're the one who brought him here."

"You have no right to do this, Lillian. You abandoned him."

"We'll let the courts decide that and see who comes out ahead."

Lillian turned to walk away.

"You don't want to see Jonathan?" Sara called out.

"No sense upsetting the child by putting him in between two bickering parents, huh, Mitch? Things could get ugly. I'll see you in Baltimore."

It had taken every ounce of control to keep from losing his temper, Mitch thought. It wouldn't solve anything. And he knew, even as Lillian drove off the Double T Ranch last night, that she was coming back. She wasn't done playing games with him.

"What are you going to do?" Sara asked quietly.

He heaved a heavy sigh and closed his eyes. "Go to Baltimore and let the judge know that a woman like Lillian has no right raising a kid. Not my kid, anyway."

"Don't you think you're being a little unfair?"

"What? How unfair is it to come back after two months and say she wants him back? Until when? She's got a reason for doing this and it has nothing to do with loving Jonathan."

He started walking back to the main house to get his son. He needed to hold him. Needed to know he was still safe here with him even though he could see the red taillights of Lillian's car bounding through the front gate of the ranch.

When had his love for his son grown so that he felt a rage of emotion in protecting him from his own mother? But it had. Sara had seen that it was possible. In her woman's way, she prodded him and kept at him until the love in his heart spilled over and he couldn't help but feel strongly for Jonathan.

And Sara. She couldn't work that kind of magic without his heart spilling over for her as well.

He was vaguely aware of Sara chasing his heels.

"Mitch, you've got to think this through. I mean really think it before you do anything rash."

"What's to think about? I'll make reservations for us on a flight to Baltimore tomorrow. We'll meet with the judge, have our say and be back on a plane before you know it."

"It's not that easy."

"Sure it is. What kind of judicial system would give a child back to a mother who abandoned him?"

He heard her heavy sigh. "It happens all the time. People make mistakes."

Mitch stopped short and swung around to face Sara. "Lillian didn't make a mistake. She made a move. There's a huge difference."

"Are you so sure?"

"Yes."

"How can you be?"

"I just am."

Sara threw her hands up in frustration. "And that

makes it alright, denying her from seeing Jonathan? Are you really so sure a judge is going to see it that way?"

"That's the way it was. How else can he see it?" He has to see it that way, Mitch thought with a groan. He would not lose his son. Not now, not ever. Jonathan would not be used as a pawn in one of Lillian's games.

"She made a mistake, Mitch."

He turned around, saw that his haste and wide strides had put him a good fifteen feet ahead of Sara. He also saw tears filling her eyes. Sad tears, different from the ones that welled in her eyes when she was telling a happy story.

He met her halfway before speaking again. "What are you saying, Sara?"

"Lillian might not have wanted to keep Jonathan for any number of reasons. Maybe she really believed she couldn't handle him or be a good mother to him. I don't know what her reasons are. I don't know her. You'll have to ask her that yourself. But whatever the reason was, maybe it was just a mistake. And maybe she realizes just how big a mistake she made in letting him go like that."

"Then she's the one who made it."

"That's it? She should just pay for her mistakes for the rest of her life?"

"It shouldn't be Jonathan who pays." He started walking toward the main house again.

"But he will. Mitch, I made a mistake. Are you telling me I should pay for the rest of my life for it?"

He swung around. "This isn't about you, Sara."

"Yes, it is. In a way. I came here to help you when

you needed it. Maybe Lillian needed a hand and no one was there to help her. I know what that's like. I've been there. Maybe that's why Lillian left Jonathan here. She knew you'd be shocked. She knew you'd be angry that she didn't tell you about him. But she knew you well enough to know you'd love him and take care of him."

He didn't want to hear it. He knew Lillian, and as much as he knew Sara believed what she was saying, he also knew it wasn't possible. Lillian just wasn't that kind of woman. He was the one who'd made the mistake in thinking the woman he'd married was the same sweet girl he'd known as a kid. But he was wrong. She'd changed. He'd been blind to that.

"If things had been different and you'd known about Jonathan before he was born . . ."

He cocked his head. "What are you suggesting? That Lillian and I would still be together?"

She looked down at the ground. She'd lost a little of her strength. "If I wasn't here—"

Shaking his head, he said, "It wouldn't change a thing. I'd still want Jonathan to be with me and I'd still be sending Lillian back to Baltimore, alone. I know Lillian. She doesn't do anything unless it benefits her in some way. She's got an ace in the hole somewhere and she's just waiting for the right time to play her hand."

"Maybe she's changed."

"No one can change that much."

A tear streamed down her cheek. "Why is it so hard for you to think she hasn't changed and yet . . ." She swiped her cheek and started walking away from him toward the foreman's house.

"Sara?"

She didn't stop walking, so he changed directions and followed her.

"Where are you going?"

"Back to the reservation, like I should have done all along."

"You can't do that. I . . ." It was hard to say the words. He needed her. It wasn't the same as it had been the first day Jonathan had come to the Double T. He wasn't as inept with his son as he had been that day or the days following. But he still needed Sara. Sara. No one else. His hands started shaking.

"What, Mitch? You need me?"

He widened his strides and caught up to her quickly, bracing her with his hands to keep her from going any further. "Yes, I do."

Her smile was bittersweet. "You know how to take care of Jonathan now."

"I'm not talking about Jonathan."

Her expression broke his heart. "Mitch, when I left Dave the first time, he destroyed me. I checked into a hotel room and found out the next day from the hotel manager that Dave had cancelled my credit card. I picked myself up only to find that he'd withdrawn all the money we had in our bank accounts. I had nothing. So I went to some friends we'd had for years . . ." Her voice cracked. "They turned me away. All my friends suddenly became *Dave's* friends and I was just a bitter soon-to-be ex-wife trying to get whatever she could from him. Even my housekeeper refused to let me into our home after Dave had the locks changed and threatened to fire her."

Mitch reached for Sara. He'd had no idea it had

been that hard for her to break free of her husband's cruelty. All he wanted to do was wrap her in his arms and tell her she didn't have to endure that pain anymore. But when he moved closer, Sara took a wide step back and knotted her arms across her chest.

"He convinced me to come back and I felt I had no choice."

"I had no idea."

"No one did. I felt too ashamed to tell anyone about it," she said, head held high.

"I'm so sorry for what you had to go through."

"Maybe Lillian felt that kind of desperation. People get stuck in situations sometimes and don't know how to get out of them." Sara sighed. "Lillian made a mistake. I know what it's like to make a mistake. And if you can't believe that she could change, then you'll never believe that I have."

"I know a thing or two about mistakes, too, Sara."

She took a step forward then, swiping her cheeks with both hands. "All the more reason you should understand. If I can change and you can, why can't Lillian?"

He shook his head. "No matter what you say, you're not like Lillian. You don't scheme and lie."

She dropped her hands to her sides in defeat. "Then you haven't been paying attention. Because when you look at Lillian's face and I see all that hate you have for what she's doing, you might as well be looking at me. The things I did to get away from Dave weren't any better than what Lillian is doing. That kind of desperation forces you to do things you'd never do otherwise. I knew the only way to get away from him was to play his game. So I did. And none of the things

I did made me feel proud. It only fueled the idea in peoples' minds that I was a spiteful soon-to-be-ex-wife."

"Is that true?"

She staggered before his eyes, clearly thrown by his questions, but quickly recovered. "They didn't know what went on behind closed doors. It was the only way to get away. Dave had a way of tearing down my spirit, cornering me relentlessly. I blamed myself as much as him for it. He wanted to destroy me so that I had no confidence that I could make it without him. And for a long time, I actually believed him. At the time, I didn't think I had anyone to turn to."

It was the first time Sara had admitted to what Mitch had suspected all along. Mitch was infinitely glad her ex-husband was far away in another state where Mitch couldn't unleash his anger on him.

"Would you do it again?"

"Things are different now. I'm different. But given the same circumstances, yes, if I had to," she said quietly.

"Good," he said, taking another step closer to her, hoping she wouldn't run away.

He wanted her in his arms so he could comfort her. But he'd let her make that move when she was ready. Right now, she looked so fragile, he was afraid she'd break if he so much as touched her.

"That still doesn't make you like Lillian. She had choices, you didn't. That makes you a survivor. You're not going to be a victim. I admire you for that, Sara. I really do. Because surviving just happens to be something I know a lot about myself. You can't keep hating yourself for doing what you had to do to get away from an abusive ex-husband."

"I can't help but think that Lillian regrets giving up her son."

A muscle in his jaw jumped. "He's my son, too. She didn't even tell me about him. She was going to give him away without me even knowing he existed. When I finally found out about him, I didn't abandon him."

He remembered that desperate feeling the moment Corrine had told him Lillian left Jonathan for him to raise. How desperate he felt and the initial urge to run right back to Baltimore to confront Lillian.

Sara stared at him for a long moment, and he sighed. Part of him wanted to know what thoughts she kept behind the depths of her dark eyes. There was suddenly such sadness there, he wanted to wipe it away. He wanted to drag her into his arms and wanted her to know that all the ugliness of her life in L.A. was too far away to touch them now. He wanted her comfort too, her gentle voice to soothe him, her tender hand to keep him steady.

But he kept his distance. Because he knew that those secrets she held tight to her were not words he wanted to hear.

"If you can't stand by me on this, Sara, then maybe you shouldn't come to Baltimore."

He forced the words past the lump in his throat, wanting to snatch them back or have her say that yes, she would stand by him. When had he come to need her so? He hadn't needed anyone in such a long time. Now when it mattered the most, he didn't want to need anyone. He wanted to stand up for his son like his parents never seemed to do for him. He wouldn't fail Jonathan that way.

Her bottom lip trembled. "If that's the way you feel."

She turned and walked back to the foreman's house. His home. He had the strangest feeling that when he returned with Jonathan, Sara would already be gone.

Sara hadn't expected the deluge of tears. At least not that many of them. But they came just the same.

It was worse somehow than the first time. When she'd known her marriage to Dave was really over, she'd begun the slow and painful process of ending things. First step, letting go of the relationship. Second step, looking at her part in all of the mistakes. Third step, letting go of the blame.

She wasn't sure she'd quite come to terms with that one. But in time, hopefully she would. Each step was as important as the one before and none could be skipped over. She kept moving forward until she was one step closer to having the courage to actually leave him.

In the end, there were no tears. No wracking sobs that tore at her soul. But as she drove down the long road leading to her mother's home on the reservation, there were tears. For Jonathan, for Mitch, and for herself.

She'd fallen in love with Mitch, despite knowing in advance that it was absolutely the last thing she should do. The heart listens to no one, her mother had once said. Hers certainly hadn't listened. She'd walked in with eyes wide open this time and given her heart away, even knowing she'd be hurt in the end.

This had been her goal. Coming home. All the way home. And she'd failed.

The car rolled to a stop in front of the house she'd grown up in and fled from. It hadn't been her home in a long time. The porch light was on and it would be shut off at nine o'clock on the nose, regardless of whether everyone was home or not, to conserve electricity. Even in the absence of daylight, Sara saw crisp white sheets clipped to a long clothesline out back, something her mother did each and every day. Some things never change here at home or on the reservation. Just one more reason she couldn't wait to leave when she was younger.

Maybe she hadn't been fair. Things had changed for all of them. Her mother's jet-black hair was streaked with age. It was beautiful on her now, Sara realized. She thought of all the times she'd religiously colored and cut her own hair to keep it looking more sophisticated. And yet, her mother had worn the same hairstyle and grown into a more beautiful and graceful woman because of it. She someone missed that lesson in life while she was here the first time. Maybe all young people did.

She jammed the car into park in the driveway and turned the ignition off.

She was home. But it wasn't. Not really. Home wasn't in L.A., not here on the reservation. Where *was* it, she wondered as she pushed through the screen door and caught her mother's bewildered expression.

Alice glanced down at the suitcase Sara had hastily packed before leaving as she plopped it down on the floor.

"Do you mind if I stay here?" she asked, knowing full well her mother would never turn her away.

Alice nodded and immediately opened her arms. It was there that Sara let her well of tears run dry.

The house was quiet. *Too quiet*, Mitch thought as he rocked back and forth in the rocker in Sara's room. He hadn't gotten around to moving Jonathan's crib into his own room. Now he sat in the dark, staring at the rise and fall of his son's chest as he slept peacefully. Selfish as it was, he wished Jonathan would wake up. He didn't want to be alone.

Fear had settled itself good and deep just beneath the surface of his composure. It had been a long time since he'd felt this way. He thought time had erased most of the scared little boy he'd been. But he was there still, buried inside the man Mitch had become. Now he showed his face again. And he was terrified.

He wanted Sara. He needed her . . .

In the still darkness, Mitch chuckled wryly. Yes, he needed Sara. As much as he didn't want to, he did.

Oh, he knew he'd get along just fine with Jonathan on his own. Sara had seen to that. But this was something different. He needed the woman, needed her quiet strength, her tender touch, and the gentle sound of her voice to ease this burden of fear threatening to consume him.

Her voice. Lord, he could hear her voice in his mind talking softly to him, echoing in the room and halls of this house.

It wasn't just his house anymore. A family lived here. Jonathan and Sara had moved not only into his house, but also into his life. He couldn't imagine being without either one of them.

His goals were still firmly in place. He'd have his own ranch one day. Except now things had taken on a new dimension. His life wasn't just about him or what he wanted. It wasn't his life or his home. It was their home. And he was so terribly afraid he'd be left behind without either one of them.

Lillian wanted Jonathan back. And Sara had left. Good God, the house seemed so empty without her. He dragged his hand across his face and rocked hard out of the chair to a stand, leaving the rocking chair to swing back and forth in the wake of his force.

He stared down at his son and felt emotion well up deep in his chest, squeezing it until he couldn't breathe.

What a revelation to come to. He'd spent most of his adult life believing he didn't need anyone but himself. Like Sara, he was a survivor. Now after a few short months, Sara had crept into his heart and he couldn't get her out. More importantly, he didn't want her out.

Jonathan stirred and murmured in his sleep and a bittersweet smile tugged at the corners of Mitch's mouth. He loved this little boy. His boy. Lord Almighty, he couldn't lose his son. He couldn't bear it. He could only imagine what might happen to him at the hands of Lillian.

Deep down, he knew it wasn't love for Jonathan that was driving Lillian. He'd been blinded by her before, but now he knew better. He had to fight. He didn't know any other way. And if he had to do it alone, then so be it. He wanted Sara, but he'd stand alone if he had to. He'd done it his whole life.

Chapter Ten

Mitch had taken the truck to the airport himself. Beau had offered to drive him, but since Mandy was due any day, Mitch didn't feel right taking him from home. Beau needed to be with Mandy even though there were a string of people at the Double T to help her along if she went into labor.

He parked the car and unbelted Jonathan's car seat from the front of the truck. It was going to rain. Even though the sun was still bright in the sky, Mitch could smell it in the air. A slight rumble of thunder rolled off in the distance where a puff of clouds was brewing. The plane would be in the air before the bad weather reached them.

A hat sat cock-eyed on Jonathan's head, protecting him from the wind. He was kicking up a storm in his car seat, jabbering and drooling like he always did. A happy baby.

It tore at Mitch's heart as he carried his son through the airport.

With Jonathan strapped inside, Mitch placed the car seat on the floor at his feet as he talked to the ticket agent.

"I made a reservation last night. I was told I could pick up the tickets here."

The woman smiled, still looking at her computer screen instead of meeting Mitch's eyes. "Name?"

"Broader. Mitchell."

"To Baltimore via Dallas/Fort Worth."

"Yes, that's right."

The agent glanced over at him for the first time. "And the baby?"

"I have him in the car seat."

Behind the ticket counter stood a standing oscillating fan whipping back and forth across the ticket agent's back. With each sweep, a fluff of her hair lifted and fell back into place as she stamped and enveloped two tickets. She handed them to Mitch.

"You can leave your luggage here and just take your carryon bag. They're loading now."

Since it was easier to hold the car seat and diaper bag without his luggage, Mitch agreed. "Thank you."

The walk across the tarmac was hot and sticky, humidity from the coming rain blanketing them. Down the runway another plane was taking off, its shadow as it flew overhead swept across the ground, catching Jonathan's eyes.

Mitch smiled at the hugeness and wonder he saw in

his son's eyes as Jonathan searched for the source of the shadow and noise.

Searches, discovery. Father and son did both in different ways. Jonathan searched for and discovered new objects to learn and grow. Mitch searched for answers and discovered he didn't have them.

Mitch stepped inside the plane and was immediately bathed in the coolness of the cabin. He handed the flight attendant his tickets.

Polished and pressed in her crisp powder-blue blouse and navy skirt, the woman smiled as she handed him his stubs. "You'll need to store the diaper bag in the over head compartment before lift-off. But if you heed anything, you can take it back down after the seat belt light goes off."

"When will we be leaving?"

"In about five minutes. You have plenty of time to settle both of you in."

She glanced down at Jonathan, giving him a wide grin as she brushed her red-tipped finger across his cheek. She was rewarded with a drooly, toothless grin and a wave of an equally drooly fist.

Laughing, she said, "Enjoy your flight."

Pulling off his straw hat, Mitch hoisted Jonathan's car seat high to avoid hitting anything or anyone, and carefully navigated the narrow aisle. He stopped short when he got to his seat number.

His pulse thrummed hard. "What are you doing here?"

Sara offered him a quick smile, but it instantly faded.

"I thought . . . it would be easier for Jonathan to stay with me while you're in court."

She sat across from him on the single-seated side of the plane. He and Jonathan occupied the twin seats opposite her. He strapped Jonathan into the seat by the window before standing up and placing the diaper bag in the overhead compartment.

When he was done, he took his seat and said, "My mother offered to watch Jonathan for me when I go to court."

His heart was filled with longing to reach out to Sara, touch her silky black hair, stroke his thumb across the planes of her smooth skin. He loved this woman, yet he couldn't bring himself to tell her how pleased he was that she was there right now. *Lord, she was here with him.* That empty feeling that had weighed him down all night and all day had lifted.

Sara simply nodded. The light in her eyes had faded some, but not her determination. Mitch could see it. He dropped his hat in his lap and fiddled with it to give his hands something to do.

Sara leaned forward and peeked at Jonathan.

"It may be easier to have me watch the baby and have your mother go to court with you. For support, I mean."

"I don't . . ." He was about to say he didn't need his mother. He didn't need anyone. It had been an automatic response most of his life. His adult life anyway. And for the most part, it had been true. Until a few months ago. Now he knew he needed someone. He needed that special someone.

"I'm going to Baltimore, Mitch," Sara said, her voice filled with determination. "I'm going."

He waited a second, tried to find the words so he

wouldn't trip over his tongue or his pride or his stupidity.

"Okay." His voice was low and thick and threatened to crack.

Minutes later, they were speeding down the runway, wheels lifting into air like the feet of a hawk. He didn't know which one of them had made the move, but their fingers met and entwined, clinging together over the aisle. His eyes sought out Sara's and found instead that she was staring straight ahead. But her face, strong and sure, held a hint of a smile he felt deep in his heart.

The taxi passed rows of triple-decker homes before turning down Maple Street. Didn't every city have a Maple Street that looked just like this? Probably, Mitch mused as he took in the sight of his old neighborhood.

They'd been cleaning it some, he thought, recalling the changes from his last visit about a year ago. Fresh paint, new porches, and patches of green turf brightened up the neighborhood in a way he hadn't thought possible. Mitch didn't often think about Baltimore when he was out at the Double T. Steerage Rock had been his home for his whole adult life. This was just a place he had lived in his youth.

Beside him, Jonathan blew saliva bubbles and giggled at himself as he discovered his own voice. Sara had been quiet.

A grin instantly split his cheeks when he saw his mother standing on the porch in her cleaning duster while she talked to Mrs. Santini, who stood on the porch in the next house. More gossip and news traveled that distance than the miles they'd traveled to get here.

Cynthia Broader's eyes caught site of the yellow taxi and squealed mid-sentence.

"They're here!" she screamed, then turning to Mrs. Santini, she added, "Oh, Claire, you just have to hold off watching your soap long enough to come meet my grandbaby with me."

" 'Course I will. They'll just be dragging things out for weeks before anything new happens anyway. Besides, I set the VCR as soon as you told me Mitchell was coming home."

Laughing, Mrs. Santini gathered up her skirt and trotted down the porch steps with as much grace as a woman her size could. Overweight by some one hundred pounds, Mrs. Santini had been Mitch's salvation on more occasions than he could remember. Cynthia and Claire had lived across a patch of grass for over thirty years and it didn't seem likely that would change until death took one of them.

"Hi, Ma. Mrs. Santini," Mitch said, tossing the driver the fare and tip before stretching out of the taxi.

Cynthia Broader had been on her own six years now. Mitch respected his mother for all she had done to get her life together, to finally break free from her abusive relationship with his father. It had taken a while for the resentment of his childhood to wear thin, but they'd managed to patch the somewhat stable relationship that had been too rocky for him as a child.

"Let me see him, Mitchell." His mother fluttered her hands and giggled like a schoolgirl as she danced on the sidewalk, waiting to meet her grandson for the first time. Mitch obliged by taking Jonathan right out of the car seat and handing him to his grandmother's waiting arms.

"Oh, would you just look at those blue eyes, Cindy," Claire said.

"Why, he's the spitting image of his daddy. Aren't you, Jonathan?" Cynthia said, tears filling her eyes.

Sara cast a wry glance at Mitch and he shrugged. "He's a good-looking kid," he whispered teasingly.

She smacked him on the shoulder playfully and retrieved the car seat while Mitch grabbed the luggage the taxi driver had deposited on the curb.

Cynthia and Claire were in a world of their own, carrying on and on as they brought the baby into the house.

"I've got your old room cleaned out just nice, Mitch. And Claire let me borrow the day crib she uses when her Mary comes over with the twins. It'll do for a bed for Jonathan until I can get one of my own."

"You won't have much use for it if he's going to be living in Texas, Cindy. It's a waste of money. You can just borrow this one anytime. It'll give me an excuse to come over and see the baby myself."

"Since when do you need an excuse?"

"I don't want to have to wait for an invitation."

"And when did you ever need one of those? Heavens to Betsy, we live on each other's doorstep. You'll know as soon as I do when he's coming for a visit."

Cynthia paraded the baby through the dining room, talking sweetly in a high-pitched, singsong voice reserved for doting grandmothers. "Now I can spoil my own grandbaby instead of having to share Claire's."

Mrs. Santini had noticed Sara first. Mitch figured it would take at least a half hour for his mother, in her joy, to notice that a woman got out of the taxi with him and the baby. But Mrs. Santini had hawk eyes and did nothing to hide her appraisal of Sara.

"I know you're not the baby's momma," she said directly.

Sara held out her hand. "Sara Lightfoot. I'm Jonathan's nanny."

Mrs. Santini's mouth twisted into a knowing grin. "Uh-huh. Nanny." Ignoring Sara's extended hand, she squeezed Sara into her ample chest for an embrace. "In this house we don't do formalities," she said, winking at Mitch.

"You didn't mention Sara coming with you," Cynthia said as she came across the carpeted floor toward them. "It was nice of you to come all this way for Mitch."

"I thought it would be easier . . . since the baby knows me."

Cynthia nodded and smiled bright. "Claire, you take hold of Jonathan for a minute while I dig up some pictures of Mitch as a baby. But don't you think you're not going to give him right back to me when I find them."

"I'll give him back alright as long as I get a good minute with this baby. Then I'll leave you alone to enjoy him all to yourself."

Mitch groaned and dropped his straw hat on the coffee table. "Ma, we don't have to drag all that out now."

"Yes, we do," Sara said quietly, tossing him a wicked grin.

He shook his head of the lightheaded feeling, but it remained. This wasn't what he'd imagined his homecoming being like. The craziness, the joy of it. But Mitch did welcome it, because it kept the fear that had nagged at him throughout the last twenty-four hours at bay.

When Cynthia returned, Mitch got straight to the point.

"Lillian mentioned a will for Grandpa."

His mother cast him a hard glance he'd seen more than a few times as a kid when he knew he was in trouble. "Not now, Mitchell. I don't want to be talking about such things while I'm enjoying my only grandchild for the first time."

She plopped a photo album in front of him on the coffee table, then sat in the center of the sofa.

"Now Sara, you sit yourself right here on the other side of me. Claire, are you going to hold that baby all day or are you going to give his Grandma a turn?"

"Oh, all right. He's just as precious as can be."

"I know."

Mrs. Santini handed the baby over to Cynthia and said her good-byes, saying she had meatballs and sauce on the stove and a tray of lasagna in the oven when everyone was hungry.

They spent a few minutes turning pages and laughing over pictures that had gone gray and fallen out of places where tape didn't hold them anymore. Happy times, Mitch thought. These pictures told only the story of the happy times.

He supposed it was good. He didn't really need to remember the moments after these snapshots were taken when booze and anger got the better of his father. Happy times were best kept on these Polaroid pictures. The rest he could forget.

"I didn't know about the will, Mitch," Cynthia finally said. "Seems your daddy dug it up before your grandpa passed on but kept it hid. Probably because it's all yours, you know?"

It was beginning to make sense, Mitch thought, closing his eyes. "If Dad had the only copy, how did Lillian find out about it?"

Cynthia sniffed and lifted her shoulder idly. "Suppose she had someone dig it up. Don't know how she could have done it. The family just assumed there was no will. Now that one has been found . . ."

"Dad must be fit to be tied." Mitch said the words to his mother and glanced at Sara. She'd gone quiet, not even looking at the pictures anymore.

"Lillian knew you were going to get a piece of something. I'm sure that's why she married you and why she's coming back now. No one dreamed your grandpa had done as well as he had in his later years. Your father is not likely to sit tight with it. I can almost guarantee he'll be fighting you for it," she warned.

"He can have it. I don't want Grandpa's money. I'm doing just fine on my own."

Cynthia snapped her eyes to him.

"Your grandpa was good to you. He knew you had dreams. Knew even more, you'd make your dreams come true if given long enough. He wanted you to have that money to make it easier for you. You take it. Your daddy won't do anything but spend it on sin or gamble it away anyway."

Sara got up from the sofa and took Jonathan from Cynthia's arms. "I should change his diaper," she said quietly.

"There's no need to run from the room, Sara, dear. This is just family talk," Claire said, dropping her now empty hands into her lap. "Why don't you let me do it? I've been waiting a lot of years to be able to fuss over a grandchild. Why don't you just sit here with Mitch and he'll give you a good look at some of these pictures."

"Okay," Sara said, handing Jonathan back to Cynthia once she'd stood up. "Everything you need is right here in the diaper bag."

"It'll come back to me soon enough, though it's been a while since I've held a baby this small."

Cynthia started for the kitchen. From where he was sitting, Mitch could see her place a towel on the kitchen table and then lay Jonathan on top of it. Sara was already deep into the photo album when he turned his head back.

Every so often she'd linger and then chuckle before turning a page.

"When was this one taken?" she asked, pointing to a picture of a dirty-faced Mitch in a dusty cowboy hat, chaps and boots. He straddled the porch rail outside as if he'd mounted a stallion. In his hand was a jump rope he'd turned into a lasso.

"I must have been about eight then, I guess."

"You always wanted to be a cowboy?"

"Pretty much. Grandpa had moved to Texas by then. He used to send me postcards of rodeos and ranches he'd visited. He'd grown up in Dallas and once my grandmother passed away, he'd gone back to be closer to his sisters. We visited him there, my dad and I, a few times after my parents were divorced. But mostly he'd visit me here. I think he was the one who took this picture."

"Dallas is a long way from Steerage Rock. How'd you end up there?"

"Grandpa moved in with his sister and her husband when I started high school. Things were getting pretty bad with both my parents around that time and he was visiting me a lot to make sure I was okay. On his last visit, my dad stopped by and grandpa saw firsthand just how living with two parents who could barely take care of themselves could be. See, even though my parents were divorced, my dad would come around, sometimes staying with my mom for a month or two before the fighting would start all over again. He could be quite a tyrant, but mom always defended him. This was one of those times, so the next morning Grandpa packed my bags and told my mom he'd had enough. He was taking me to Texas to live with him.

"Mom cried, but I think even she knew it was best. She pretended it was only for a little while, that she was going to get some help and straighten herself out."

"And I did." Cynthia was standing in the doorway holding a clean Jonathan. Her face was unreadable and suddenly Sara felt uncomfortable having heard something so personal. "Not right away, mind you. It took me a few falls and lot of hard, scary looks in the mirror. Looking at your mistakes and trying to find your way back is never easy."

"But you did it, Ma. That's what counts. And I'm very proud of you for doing it. Not just for me, but for you."

She smiled then and a sheen of tears lit her eyes.

"My life is better now. I'm not about to go messing up a good thing a second time around."

Cynthia sighed and settled into a wing chair opposite them in the living room. "Now that we have all that out of the way, what have you decided to do about this child?"

"We go to court tomorrow. I spoke with a family lawyer on the phone before we left Texas. I'll be meeting with her before the hearing."

"Are you sure you want to go through with all this?" Cynthia said, nuzzling Jonathan. "He's such a precious child. I can't bear to think of him caught in all this squabbling. Did you try to work something out with Lillian first?"

"She wants to take him back here."

Cynthia's eyes lit brighter. "I can't say that I wouldn't be thrilled to death if you were to come back home to Baltimore. It would give me a chance to enjoy this child right. I know things are better with us these past few years, but it would give us a second chance, too, Mitch."

"In case you haven't looked around lately, Ma, there aren't a whole lot of cattle ranches for sale in Baltimore."

"Maybe not in Baltimore. But there are places closer. It doesn't have to be Texas. You could still have yourself a ranch and be closer to home. Have you thought about that?"

Sara watched Mitch as he mulled it over. It would make things easier for Jonathan to have both parents close by. But, it would shut her out of his life completely and she selfishly didn't want that.

It was then that he glanced at Sara and she knew the thought had crossed his mind.

"It's a possibility. But I'm not making a move until the time is right. I'm not in any position to buy a spread just yet."

"If you take your inheritance into consideration, you are. Mitch, your father and I spent the better part of our marriage and years beyond fighting about anything and everything. And if it meant using you to get to the other, we did it."

It didn't take a great deal of thinking to know that it had taken a lot for Cynthia to admit that and that it hurt. She gazed down at her grandson with deep love and regret etched in her smile.

"I don't want this darling baby caught in a tug of war and hurt the way you were."

"I'm not like Dad. I'm trying to keep Jonathan from getting hurt."

Cynthia's laugh was bittersweet. "Honey, we all think we're doing things in the best interest of the child. Yet, somewhere along the way, we start believing that our way is the only way and the only one who ends up really hurt is the child. I thank God and your grandpa for helping to break this miserable cycle. The fact that you have turned your life into something positive is testament to someone else's caring of your best interest."

"Lillian—"

With a wave of her hand, Cynthia cut him off. "Never mind Lillian. Think of Jonathan. Who are you really doing this for?"

* * *

Mitch slept very little that night. It wasn't only the court hearing that he worried over. He worried about what was going to happen to all of them.

He hadn't really given Lillian a chance, he admitted. Maybe that was what Sara had been so upset about. He'd been so afraid of losing Jonathan and so bent on making sure that Lillian didn't hurt him that he was blinded to how controlling he'd been. He wasn't much better than Sara's ex-husband on that matter.

They hadn't had a chance to really talk about it. There had been time on the plane and in the taxi ride over to his mother's house. But Mitch hadn't wanted to face his own feelings here.

He knew it had to weigh heavy on Sara's mind, but she didn't push. When she was ready, she'd speak her mind again, let him know exactly how she felt. She wasn't one to keep her feelings hidden and it was something he admired about her. There were no games. He liked that. More important, he needed that.

At three A.M. he paced down to the kitchen and pulled out the orange juice, drinking it directly from the carton.

"I hope you don't do that back at the ranch."

Mitch spun around and in the dim light coming from the lit match in her hand, he saw Sara. She touched the wick of the candle that was placed in front of her on the table and an amber glow filled the space around them. The smell of the spent match she'd blown out and the burning wax filled the air. Sara sat at the kitchen table in her cotton bathrobe just staring up at him.

"I didn't realize anyone else was awake," Mitch said.

"I got up just a few minutes before you came down. I couldn't sleep either." She leaned over and pulled the chair out from the table. "Join me?"

He put the carton of juice back in the fridge and joined her at the table. Instantly she placed her hand over his as he propped them on the table. They sat there in the quiet of the night.

"What's the candle for?"

"A prayer."

He nodded. He knew so little about Sara's culture. How could he possibly know what it meant to her if he knew nothing about it?

"*Zee tsa lit ni'*, a friendship prayer," she continued quietly. She continued her prayer, speaking softly in her native language, her dark eyes closed to him. When she was done, she gave his hand a squeeze.

"That was nice," he said, lamely, not understanding a word of what she'd said.

She chuckled softly. "Technically, the rite should be performed by a medicine man or a very close blood relative. But Jonathan can't talk yet."

She glanced at him as he stared at her.

Her lips tilted to a grin. "That was a joke."

He nodded.

"It's a prayer of lifelong protection from evil."

Mitch nodded his understanding then. "I'm going to need it then."

"It's going to be okay, you know," Sara said, wishing she'd believe it herself if she said it enough.

"I . . . I'm scared." It was a small voice, deep and strong, but so very small at the same time. Sara wondered how many times Mitch had sat in this house in the dark and said those words. He'd come so far from the little boy who'd been hurt here. So much had happened and yet, here he was again, feeling the same pain.

"I know you are. I am, too."

"But you still think I'm wrong."

"I don't think you're wrong, Mitch. I just don't think you've thought it through. Jonathan isn't a piece of property to be divided up. He's a child who needs his mother."

"He needs a mother. But just because Lillian claims the title, doesn't mean she'll be one."

"Maybe. Maybe not. I don't know her like you do."

He sighed. "It's the money she wants."

"Did she say that?"

"In a roundabout way. She said she wanted Jonathan to get all that was coming to him."

"Any mother would want everything they could give their child." Sara rubbed her eyes with her other hand and dropped it to the table. "Did you ask her, Mitch?"

"What?"

"The reason she left him."

"I asked her why she didn't tell me about him."

"Why don't you ask her why she left him? Then maybe you'll understand the reason she wants him back."

He played with her fingers in the dark, caressing them, sending a flow of sensation through her body.

"Mitch, you have to think about what you'll do if the judge gives Jonathan back to her." It broke Sara's heart to say it aloud. She knew Mitch had to have been thinking about what Cynthia had said about moving closer to Baltimore, but he hadn't said a word. If he wasn't awarded custody, he could always try to get joint custody or visitation and see Jonathan on a regular basis. That was near impossible if he was living in Steerage Rock.

"Mitch?"

"I can't lose my son," he said quietly. "And I won't abandon him."

That said it all. He didn't have to say anymore.

"You should get some sleep," she said. Getting to her feet, she blew out the candle and pulled her hand from his, wanting nothing more than to run so she could find a quiet corner and cry.

"Sara?"

She made it to the doorway and looked back. "What is it?"

"Why did you come with me to Baltimore? Even after the way I treated you the other night."

"You said you needed me. And I'm your friend."

He started to say something, hesitated, then said, "Will you come with me to court? I don't know if I can . . . do this alone." His voice broke. In the light of the moon shining through the window above the sink, she saw his jaw tighten and his eyes close. She wanted to reach out to him, to wrap her arms around his shoulders and tell him that she'd always be there for him. He didn't have to do this alone.

But something held her back, keeping her from reaching out to him and telling him what was in her heart. Good Lord, she loved him. After tomorrow, their lives would take a very dramatic turn. If Mitch lost custody of Jonathan, he'd be leaving Steerage Rock and coming back east to be with his son.

And she'd be going to live on the reservation without him.

Her heart was torn. Yes, she loved him. But it was clear that loving him would only end up hurting her in the end.

She walked over to the table and as she did, he rose to his feet. She instantly melted into his embrace, took from him the comfort he gave while giving it back.

This is love, she thought. Something she had never had in her marriage to Dave. Never had her husband opened himself up so vulnerably, trusting in her to be there for him. She buried her head in the crook of Mitch's neck, felt his heartbeat hammer against the walls of his chest as he stroked her hair.

"I'm going to talk to Lillian before we go into court," he whispered.

She closed her eyes and waited for Mitch to continue.

"If it means moving back east to make this work . . ."

"I know," she said in a far away voice.

"Thank you."

She pulled back, gazing up at him in the moonlight, and she fought mightily to keep from breaking down. This wasn't about her and Mitch. He was doing this for Jonathan. "For what?"

He tipped her chin up with his fingers, grazing his rough, calloused hand along her jaw, making her head spin. "For being my friend. I don't think I've ever had a true friend like you."

Tears sprang to her eyes. "Neither have I."

He kissed her lips and lingered there. Her head spun in circles and she clung to him to keep herself steady.

Yes, she was steady with Mitch in a way she hadn't been on the reservation or in L.A. And it had nothing to do with where she was. It was who she was when she was with Mitch.

After all this time, she'd finally found a man she loved and a friend like no other.

She was going to lose both.

Chapter Eleven

"You want what?"

Lillian stood in front of them outside the downtown courthouse, her arms crossed in front of her, her perfectly made-up face smug. "You heard me, Mitch."

"That's blackmail."

"You want to keep the baby, you need to pay me to stay out of his life."

"So all this crap about wanting him back was a lie?" Sara shot back. She took a step forward, but Mitch held her back with his outstretched arm.

It shouldn't have shocked Sara so, but it did. Mitch had been right. Lillian had been using Jonathan as a ploy to extort money from Mitch. Knowing Mitch as she did, Lillian had to know he would fall in love with his son and pay any price to keep him.

"You can start by writing out a check for half now."

Mitch squeezed Sara's hand a little too tightly before he caught himself and let go. No doubt he was trying to keep his anger in check after Lillian's revelation.

"How did you know about the will?"

She quirked an eyebrow. "Does it really matter?"

"It does to me."

She sighed impatiently. "I met your dear dad in Atlantic City, not long before you and I were involved. He told me about the will over the blackjack table and a bottle of scotch."

Mitch's face registered pure shock, but Sara's shock had turned to betrayal. How could she have been so wrong about Lillian?

"Before we married," he said tightly. His laugh was bitter and hard. "You and my old man?"

Lillian scowled. "Please! I recognized your father and struck up a conversation with him. Your father probably doesn't even remember meeting me or what he told me. And even if he did, it's his loss and my gain."

"Does it end here? Or are you going to keep coming back to extort more money from me?"

Lillian grinned. "That depends."

"On what?" Sara said, outraged.

"On how much money is actually in that will, of course."

Mitch laughed again. "You haven't even seen the will yet, have you? For all I know my grandfather left me his antique gumball machine and World War Two memorabilia. Anything of his is priceless to me, but I don't think you'd see it quite the same way. I'll take my chances in court."

Lillian's face hardened. "I'd think long and hard about that before you do."

"When the judge hears what I have to say—"

"It won't matter when I present him with my proof."

Mitch stopped short. His hand found Sara's again and he squeezed it.

"That's right," Lillian taunted. "You didn't think I'd have gone to the trouble of bringing you all the way back here if I didn't have proof for my case, now did you?"

"What proof could be more damaging than the fact that you left a baby on my doorstep with no word of when you'd be coming back?"

She smiled sweetly. "How about hotel receipts in Steerage Rock proving that I was living there all along?"

"If you were in Steerage Rock all that time, why didn't you come back sooner?" Sara asked.

"It would have ruined my plans."

"A single hotel receipt isn't enough proof. You could have picked it up from anyone staying in the area. It doesn't mean you were there," Mitch charged.

"Well, then there are the telephone records showing I called the ranch on several occasions, only to have my calls refused."

"But you never . . . oh, directions to the powwow," Sara said, recalling the longer than normal conversation. "And those wrong numbers. That was all you?"

Lillian nodded. "When I'm done telling the judge that I sent Jonathan to meet his father only to be turned away and driven to taking legal action to get him back, you'll see who wins."

Sara stepped forward. "How could you do that? Don't you even care about Jonathan?"

"He's a darling kid," Lillian said, shifted uncomfortably for a moment before straightening her spine. "But in case you haven't noticed, I'm not exactly mother material. I never intended to raise a kid."

"You only intended to use one for money," Sara supplied.

"Let's go," Mitch said, pulling her toward the court. "My lawyer is here."

Furious and unable to find her voice, Sara twisted on her heels where she and Mitch met his lawyer.

As Liz Chadwick introduced herself to both of them, Sara felt sick inside. And angry that she'd actually felt empathy for Lillian to the point of almost ruining her relationship with Mitch.

"Are we ready to go inside?" Liz asked as she reached them.

Mitch gazed at her and then to Lillian as she breezed by them on her way into the courthouse.

"No," he sighed and proceeded to fill Liz in on the conversation they'd just had with Lillian. "There isn't anything we can do?"

The lawyer just shook her head of tight curls, pulling off her wire-rimmed glasses. "No matter what you say about her character, the evidence is damaging. It looks as though she's been in Texas all this time. The phone calls to the ranch, the hotel receipts. It all makes it look like she didn't abandon Jonathan at all. I'd say it's more damaging to you."

Mitch blew out a frustrated breath, his jaw tight

with fury. "That's not the way it happened. The only reason she's doing this is for money."

"Maybe so, but she's got the cards stacked in her favor. We have no proof except the word of a father, who as the evidence indicates, has tried to keep his son from his mother." As Liz wiped her glasses clean with a tissue, she sighed. "We'll just have to hope the judge is open-minded enough to hear us out. I'll meet you inside in five minutes."

"Don't worry," Sara said, smiling up at him. What else could she do? But it didn't have the desired effect.

"How can you say that? I don't know how I'm going to fight against this."

She wrapped her arms around his shoulders and reached up on her toes, giving Mitch a kiss. "You're going to walk into that court and tell the judge the truth. That you love your son and you have his best interest at heart."

"What does that mean for us?" His gaze was so intense, she didn't know what to say.

"We'll worry about that later. You'll see. Everything is going to be just fine."

This was Mitch's fight and he needed to do it his way, Sara thought, her heart pounding as they climbed the courthouse stairs. She was here as Mitch's friend, to support him in any way he needed. Whatever the outcome might be.

The courtroom was filled with people waiting to be heard. Mitch had never seen the inside of a courtroom, except on TV. It didn't look very much like the docudrama's he'd seen and suddenly he had no idea what to expect.

"They'll be hearing some other cases before ours," his lawyer said as they sat down.

The wait was long and tedious. Mitch tried his best not to show his nervous energy.

"Will the parties *Broader vs. Broader* please step up to the bench," the judge finally asked.

Lillian had just stepped into the courtroom, led by her lawyer. He was polished to a spit shine, complete with an Armani suit.

Sara sat in her seat while Mitch rose with his lawyer. He glanced back at her before joining Lillian and the lawyers in front of the judge.

"I've read the affidavits and I have to admit cases like this anger me a great deal. To use a child in a marital dispute in unconscionable," said the judge.

"Your Honor, we've submitted our statement of the events that took place in Texas," Liz interjected.

"I see that, Ms. Chadwick. But it doesn't exactly mesh with the statement Mrs. Broader made."

"For the record, Lillian Devereaux changed her name to Broader only recently. On the marriage certificate and the annulment papers she chose to keep her maiden name."

"It's not uncommon to want to have the same last name as your child. I've seen it many times in divorce cases. It's not against the law to change your name to Woody the Clown if it makes you happy."

A ripple of quiet laughter broke free in the courtroom, which the judge stifled with one hard look.

"What I don't understand, Mr. Broader, is why you did not support your ex-wife during her pregnancy."

When Liz tried to answer, the judge held up a hand. "I'd like to hear it directly from Mr. Broader."

"After the annulment I immediately left for Texas. I didn't even know Lillian was pregnant with my child until she dropped Jonathan on my doorstep when he was just a few weeks old."

The judge glanced down at the papers, his eyes grazing their conflicting statements. He shut the papers quickly and pushed them aside.

"You claim she made no attempt to contact you until the night before you were served papers to bring your son home?"

"That's correct."

"Then how do you explain all the evidence to the contrary?"

"It's a lie," Mitch said flatly.

The judge drew in a deep breath and a rumble of whispers spread out in the courtroom and died. "I believe it is my job to decide that."

Pulling the papers back in front of him, he said. "It is also my job to decide where this child should be raised. I'd like to hear from both of you why you think I should choose you. We'll start with Mr. Broader."

"Because I love him," Mitch said simply. "I'm not saying I did right from the start, because I didn't. It was quite a shock to find out I was a father. But in time, and with some help—a lot of help—I fell in love with my son."

Sara listened to Mitch's declaration, his voice deep and steady when he spoke of his love for Jonathan. If for no other reason that this, it was worth all the pain of loving Mitch just to have him come to this place in his life, knowing his love for his son. Tears sprang to her eyes.

"Love alone isn't enough," the judge said. "This

child needs care. This statement states you have a nanny taking care of him while you work. But you work long hours. Mrs. Broader has stated that you are looking for another nanny."

Lillian's lawyer interjected. "With proper child support, my client can care for the infant herself and live comfortably."

"I'm aware of the kind of child support your client is seeking. We'll have to shave that down a bit to meet the state's guidelines."

"What state guidelines?" Lillian shot out.

"Child support is based on salary. The inheritance referenced here is irrelevant in child support cases. It is up to Mr. Broader to appropriate what he chooses to his son in his own will or trust."

"But what about me? I was married—"

Impatiently the judge cut her off. "And you had the marriage annulled after only two weeks. Mrs. Broader, your attorney should have explained this to you. The money was willed to your ex-husband before you were married, and he inherited it after the marriage dissolved, therefore making you ineligible to claim any of it as his spouse. If you have a problem with that, take it up with your divorce lawyer. But I can guarantee if you come before my bench with this, I will strike it down."

Steam seemed to rise from Lillian's ears. She gave a hard glance at Mitch and folded her arms across her chest.

"My primary concern is this child and the events that have transpired since his birth. I'm taking a half-hour recess to mull over these affidavits before making my decision." With the strike of his gavel, he rose and strode into his chambers.

"I had a chance to look at the evidence Lillian's lawyer has and I won't lie to you. It doesn't look good," Liz said, snapping her briefcase closed. "Why don't you two grab a cup of coffee? There is a cafeteria in the lower level. I'm going to see if there are any last-minute tricks I can pull to help us. I'll meet you back here when court reconvenes."

In silence, they took the elevator to the bottom floor. Mitch looked so shattered, it made Sara's heart ache. When the elevator door flew open, she was as surprised as Mitch to see Lillian waiting for them, a smug grin splitting her face.

Mitch stiffened.

"Have you given my offer any more thought, Mitch darling?"

"I won't bargain with you for my son."

"You're going to lose what's most precious to you. Then what?"

He didn't respond, but Sara could feel his pulse pounding where she held his arm.

"As soon as we walk into that courtroom again, it will be too late. The judge will give me custody of Jonathan and I promise you, I'm not going to make it easy for you to see him. I suggest you think about that for a while."

Lillian turned on her heels and waltzed into the ladies room.

Mitch's heavy sigh spoke the gravity of emotion he was feeling. Sara had believed this was Mitch's fight. It wasn't her place to intervene. She was here only to lend her support to him if he needed it. But she was wrong in thinking it was only about Jonathan. It was about the two of them, too. And Sara had a lot of fight in her in that regards.

"Why don't you get us something to drink? I'll be right back," she said.

"What are you doing?"

She drew in a breath of courage and smiled up at him, feeling confident for the first time in a long time. "I think it's time Lillian and I had a woman-to-woman chat."

Mitch shook his head. "I don't want you anywhere near that woman. There's no telling what she'll do."

Sara chuckled. "You don't have to protect me, Mitch. My feet are feeling pretty steady right now."

His dark brows drew together. "What are you going to do?"

"Do you trust me?"

"With my life," he said.

He gave her a crooked grin and bent his head to kiss her lips. As he drew back, he was about to say something, hesitated, then shook his head.

"Don't worry," she said, touching her hand to his cheek.

"Why don't I see if they serve any herbal teas here?"

It wasn't what he was going to say. It had been an afterthought, Sara knew. As she pushed through the restroom doors, she wondered just what it was he'd held back.

Lillian was staring at her reflection in the mirror, applying a fresh coat of lipstick as she approached.

Sara didn't waste any time getting to the point.

"Tell me something. Did you just marry Mitch to get his money?"

"What do you think?" Lillian glanced at Sara's reflection and shrugged. "Mitch is a good man."

"I won't argue with that. What about Jonathan?"

"You know what they say about the passion of wedding nights. I didn't trick him or try to trap him. After Mitch told me there was no will and that anything his grandfather had would probably go to his father, I didn't see any need to stay married to him. I mean, I wasn't going to go traipsing through manure on some cattle ranch in Texas until Mitch saved enough money to buy a ranch in some equally boring town."

Lillian was facing Sara now. "After Mitch had gone back to Texas, I realized I was pregnant. I wasn't even sure it was Mitch's baby. It didn't make any sense to tell him unless I knew for sure."

"Mitch said you were going to give him up for adoption."

Lillian's face hardened. "That's right. It would have been my choice, too. But when I saw the baby and saw how much he looked like Mitch—"

"You knew he'd do anything to keep his son. Even pay you for him?"

"I found out there actually was a will and what's more important, Mitch got it all. So I didn't go through with the adoption and I brought Jonathan to Texas."

"And waited until Mitch was so in love with his son he'd do anything to get him back. Is that how it was?"

"Something like that."

Sara held back a retort and counted to ten to calm herself. "To think I was actually on your side." Thinking about it now made her sick.

Lillian smiled. "Good, then you can help Mitch see things my way so we can stop all this silliness."

"No, I can't," Sara said, shaking her head. "And I'm sorry if that disappoints you. You see, Mitch has a mind of his own and he doesn't allow me or anyone else to control him. Nor does he control anyone else."

She reached into her purse and pulled out the small micro-cassette recorder she'd placed there that morning before she'd left Mitch's mother's house. She rewound it just enough to give Lillian a taste of what was on it.

"In case you haven't noticed, I'm not mother material—" She snapped off the cassette player.

"You little witch," Lillian said, with a twist of hate and appreciation all in one.

"It's all here. The conversation in front of the courthouse where you demanded money in exchange for Jonathan. And everything you've said just now."

"He's not going to win and neither are you."

"I wouldn't write Mitch off just yet. Once the judge hears this tape, there is no way he'll give you custody of Jonathan." It hurt Sara deep in her heart to say the words, even though she knew there was no love in Lillian's heart for the baby. She ached for Jonathan and for what he'd never had in Lillian.

"You're just like me, little Cherokee. I'm not going to let you take what is rightfully mine."

"Apache."

Lillian frowned and then rolled her eyes. "Same thing."

Standing tall, Sara replied, "That's where you are wrong. You see, Apache people are warriors. And deep in my culture are people who know how to fight for what is right. Unlike you, I'm not doing this for money. I'm doing it out of love," she said, depositing the tape in her bag.

"Before you walk into that court, I'd think a little bit about how you're going to spend any money you might be able to swindle from Mitch while you're behind bars for extortion."

Lillian's back straightened. "You can't use that tape."

"Really? Are you that sure that you're willing to take the gamble? I can walk right out this door and hand it over to the District Attorney if you'd like."

Lillian tossed her lipstick case into her purse and zipped it closed, soaring past Sara on her way to the door.

"You're Jonathan's mother," Sara said, stopping Lillian at the door. She sighed, her heart breaking for that little boy all over again. "You haven't even asked about him once. Nothing. Not how he's coming along. Not whether or not he's rolling over or . . . anything. Don't you even care?"

Lillian's lips twisted into a snarl, but it did nothing to stop Sara from speaking her piece.

"If you were doing this out of love for Jonathan, he would have been first and foremost on your mind. Mitch's money wouldn't mean a thing."

"Guess you have all the answers," Lillian snapped.

"I wish I did."

"You haven't won," Lillian bit back.

"This isn't about winning. It's about making sure a little boy gets the love he deserves from people who truly care about him."

*   *   *

The cup of coffee Mitch had downed too quickly while he waited for Sara felt like mud in the pit of his stomach.

"Don't worry," she'd said. How could he possibly not worry? In all likelihood, his son was about to be taken away from him before he even had a chance to get to know him, before he had the opportunity to grow and become his own person. He couldn't stand it and there was nothing he could do about it.

Almost immediately, the air in the courtroom changed. Mitch was having a hard time breathing and wished he could take off his noose of a tie and end his charade.

Lillian and her lawyer walked into the courtroom just as the judge approached his bench.

"If it pleases the court, I'd like to approach the bench," Lillian's lawyer asked.

"It's a little late to add any more information to this case, counselor."

"There has been a drastic . . . change of heart."

The judge scowled. "What kind of change?"

"May approach the bench?"

"Anything said at this point should be on record, Mr. Davis. If you feel you must address the court before my decision is heard then go ahead."

Mr. Davis was clearly unhappy that he was not allowed a private say, but he proceeded. "My client has decided to drop all further action against the baby's father."

"Meaning what?"

"She wishes the child to remain in the custody of Mr. Broader."

A hush swept across the room. Mitch couldn't believe what he was actually hearing. Apparently, neither could the judge.

"Say that again?"

"My client would like to relinquish all custody of her son, Jonathan Broader."

The judge pulled off his glasses and pinched the bridge of his nose. "This is highly unusual, especially at this late date in the proceedings. May I ask what has brought you to this decision?"

Lillian cleared her throat. "Mitch is a good father. I believe he can take better care of Jonathan than I can."

Judge Babcock didn't appear convinced. "I want you to think a minute before answering me. Is this decision one that you've made of your own accord?"

"Yes, Your Honor." She glanced at Mitch, her face unreadable. What was going on? What was Lillian up to now?

"And you haven't been pressured in any way?"

"No."

"I'm not sure I like this turn of events and I'm not satisfied that coercion of some sort hasn't come into play here."

When the judge turned to Mitch, his heart pumped harder than a wild horse on the run.

"Mr. Broader, I can't say that I'm still not concerned by this situation. You are the child's father and based on that will get full custody by default. There's no evidence to show you are unfit to take on that responsibility. But I'm not sure a life being raised by a nanny will enable this child to have the love he deserves. Further, having a different nanny coming in and out of his life and having a father who works the long hours that are required on a ranch doesn't give much emotional security. It's hard enough being a single parent. How do you feel you'll manage that?"

Mitch thought of Sara and all the nights she'd pushed him to bond with his son. Emotion swelled inside of him just thinking about all she'd done for them, for him.

"Well, Your Honor, that's where Lillian is wrong." He turned and glanced at Sara. "Ms. Lightfoot is more than just a nanny. She came into my life at a time when I was confused and scared witless about being a father, and she made me take the reins. She's turned a shell of a house I lived alone in into a home that is bubbling over with life."

And love, he thought. She'd filled both his heart and his home with the very essence of love.

He kept his eyes on Sara as he spoke. "I'm not looking to change things at all. I like them just the way they are, except for one thing. I'm hoping one day we'll be married and be a real family."

The judge nodded. "Answer me one thing. What if the situation hadn't turned out in your favor? Texas is a long way from Baltimore. How would you have been a father to your son then?"

"If Jonathan was here in Baltimore then I would have chosen to be near him. He means the world to me. And I can't remember what my life was like before he came into it." He shrugged. "And I would have prayed that Sara would have come with me."

That brought a smile to the judge's face. "Full custody is awarded to Mr. Mitchell Broader, the child's father." And with another stroke of the gavel, it was over.

With a sneer on her lips, Lillian sailed past him without a word. Mitch didn't want to think past his joy to wonder what had happened or what had brought it about. All he cared about was that Jonathan was going home with him. He couldn't wait to hold his son in his arms again.

He hooked his arm around Sara's and walked out of the courthouse in silence, not wanting to waste another moment in case Lillian changed her mind.

Once inside a taxi and heading to his mother's house, Sara wrapped her arms around him and kissed him on the cheek.

"Congratulations, Mitch. You must be so relieved this is over."

He kissed her back, this time on the lips. "What happened between you and Lillian to make her change her mind?"

"What makes you think I had anything to do with it?"

He cocked his head to one side. "Don't tell me you had a heart-to-heart and she miraculously realized the error of her ways."

Sara sighed, opening her purse and pulling out a small tape recorder. "Before I left Dave for good, I got smart. I told you I did despicable things that I'm ashamed of. One of them was taping his abuse and threatening to expose him, to show it to all those so-called friends who had defended him the first time I left. I had boxes of tapes when I finally went to the lawyer for my divorce."

"You blackmailed him?"

Sara closed her eyes, shame filling her. "I'm not proud of it. Even in doing it, he fought me tooth and nail during our divorce, and I felt I had no choice." She rewound the tape a little way and hit the PLAY button.

"*After Mitch told me there was no will and that anything his grandfather had would probably go to his father, I didn't see any need to stay married to him. I mean, I wasn't going to go traipsing through manure on some cattle ranch in Texas until Mitch saved enough money to buy a ranch in some equally boring town—*"

She clicked off the tape and spared Mitch the rest.

"I told Lillian I'd go to the D.A. if I had to. I'm sorry."

Mitch sighed, then chuckled, relief filling him completely. "Why? You fought fire with fire. Thank you for doing that. If you hadn't, Lillian would have gotten away with taking Jonathan and God only knows what kind of life he'd have had."

"You're not angry?"

"How could I be? If I'd had an ounce of sense, I would have known that Lillian would only respond to the same kind of treatment she dished out. She doesn't know the meaning of fair play."

He wrapped his arms around her and she settled against him, molding to his side and making him feel whole again.

"Sara, what I said in court—"

"Hmm, I wondered when you'd get to that."

"I don't want you to feel like I'm putting pressure on you to stay at the ranch. I was feeling pretty desperate in there and—"

"Did you mean what you said?"

He gazed down into her eyes, replaying in his head

his own words spoken in front of the judge just a short time ago and knowing they were true. "Yes."

"All of it?"

He smiled. "Every word. Except I forgot to say the part about how much I love you."

Tears sprang to her eyes. "Really?"

"I love you, Sara. I'm a patient man, so if you need time then I'll give it to you. If living on the reservation is what will make you happy then, I guess we can have ourselves a ranch there someday, can't we?"

"You would do that for me?"

"If it means keeping you in my life, yes."

"Mitch, do you have any idea why I came to Baltimore even after you told me not to?"

"You said it was because I needed you."

"That's right. And you know what? I needed you, too. I sat there in the house I grew up in and all I could think about was being with you and Jonathan. I couldn't imagine being anywhere else. That little house on the Double T has been more of a home to me in these last few months than all the years I spent in L.A. And I realized, it wasn't the house or the reservation that made me home. It was you. It doesn't matter where I am as long as I'm with you. And in case you're wondering, if things hadn't turned out this way, if Lillian had won, I would have chosen to be with you."

He bent his head and kissed her lightly on the lips, his heart singing. "I love you, Sara."

She chuckled softly, her dark eyes shining brightly. "I love you, too, Mitch. And don't you think for one minute I'm going to let you off the hook about marrying me."

He laughed hard and then kissed her. Oh, what a kiss. It was filled with the promise of a lifetime of love.

"I wouldn't dream of it," he said, smiling down into her deep brown eyes, watching her love for him shining back. "In fact, I might just take you back to the courthouse and marry you before you change your mind."

"Not a chance, cowboy. Let's get our son and go home."